Unraveled

Unraveled

PD Norris

CONTENTS

For my beloved sister Mattaniah, whose light was extinguished far too soon. Your spirit and laughter will forever echo in my heart, guiding me through the darkest days. May you finally get justice.

Prologue

Niyah sat in her recliner, the glow of her phone screen lighting up the room. She couldn't believe how quickly the past few months had flown by. Weeks filled with video calls, endless texts, and inside jokes that had made her feel like she'd known Malik forever. They were going to meet in person on Saturday. Her phone buzzed and she smiled, seeing his name pop up.

Niyah: So... Saturday's still on, right?

Malik: Of course. You're not backing out on me, are you?

Niyah: Lol, no way. Just can't believe we're finally meeting after all this time.

Malik: I know. I think it's about time we do this in person.

Niyah: Yeah, I'm excited... but also nervous.

Malik: Nah, don't be nervous. It's gonna be just like our calls, except we won't have to worry about bad WiFi.

Niyah: Haha, true! It just feels different, you know?

Malik: Different, but in a good way. Trust me, it'll be chill.

Niyah: I hope so. So, I'll be helping my niece move that day. You can pick me up from there.

Malik: Works for me. I'll be waiting. Just let me know where to meet you.

Niyah: I'll text you the address around the time we finish. Probably around 7.

Malik: Perfect. Can't wait to finally see you in person.

Niyah: Same here. It's gonna be fun. See you Saturday.

Chapter 1

Zara glanced down at her phone as it buzzed, signaling the incoming group text from her two aunts, Janelle and Niyah. She smiled, scrolling through their contrasting messages, each a perfect reflection of the women she'd grown up around.

Janelle's message was straightforward, as always: "Hey Zara, what time should we be there Saturday?"

Niyah's followed immediately after: "Girl, you moving already? That's wild! What should I wear? Hope you ain't making us do any heavy lifting. You know my nails just got done!"

Zara chuckled, shaking her head. If anyone knew how different the two sisters were, it was her. Janelle and Niyah were complete opposites, but somehow that never seemed to weaken their bond. In fact, it often made their family dynamic more interesting.

Janelle Norton, the younger of the two by one year, was the responsible one. She was the planner, the organizer, the voice of reason. She always kept things in order, whether it was family gatherings or just everyday life. Zara admired her aunt's strong, no-nonsense attitude, even if Janelle sometimes came across as a little too serious. She was the one who made sure things got done. Zara always thought that her aunt was the kind of woman who had her life together in every possible way.

An accomplished mental health counselor, Janelle was also deeply rooted in family. Zara could always count on her for advice, whether she wanted it or not. And though Janelle's firmness could be intimidating, there was a warmth in her that only those close to her could fully understand. She had an uncanny ability to listen without judgment, making anyone feel heard, even in the toughest of times. Her unwavering support made her the backbone of their family, always there to lend a hand or a word of wisdom when needed most.

Then there was Niyah Thompson. She was the one who was free-spirited, unpredictable, and always the life of the party. Zara couldn't imagine the family without her aunt's spontaneous energy. Where Janelle was structure, Niyah was chaos in the best possible way. She didn't work due to a disability, but her vibrant personality reflected in everything she did. Niyah could be counted on to bring laughter into even the most serious situations, always with her unique blend of wit and charm. She had a way of turning everything into a fun experience, even if it wasn't always practical.

Growing up, Zara had always felt like a bridge between the two, learning to balance the practical with the playful. She admired her aunt's determination and admired Niyah's ability to live in the moment. As the only daughter of their older sister Felicia, Zara had been doted on by both aunts since she was little. Now, at 30, she still felt their influence in every part of her life.

As Zara tapped out a response, the familiar contrast between her two aunts made her smile.

"Thanks, Nelly. Anytime after 8 works. And Aunt Niyah, don't worry, no heavy lifting for you, promise!"

Janelle's message buzzed in almost immediately: "Who's bringing breakfast?"

Niyah's responded immediately: "Not me. But I'll bring the music."

Zara shook her head with a laugh, knowing exactly what that meant. Niyah would show up fashionably late with a speaker blasting something fun and upbeat, turning what should be a stressful moving day into an impromptu dance party. Despite the chaos, Niyah's energy had a way of making everything feel lighter. Even the most tedious tasks somehow became more enjoyable when she was around, her infectious enthusiasm spreading like wildfire.

Zara's phone buzzed again as she was in the middle of packing up a box of linen. She wiped her forehead and glanced at the screen to see another message from Janelle.

"Anything specific you need the boys to do? Marcus and Jordan will be there."

Zara's face lit up at the mention of her two cousins. Marcus and Jordan were Janelle's sons, and though they were a few years younger than her, they were dependable when it came to helping with heavy lifting. Marcus was the oldest and he owned his own auto repair shop while Jordan worked as a welder. Even though Jordan was a year younger than his brother, he was an inch taller.

She quickly typed back: "Yes! I need them for the heavy stuff. I've got furniture that needs moving and no way I'm doing it alone!"

She smiled to herself as she sent the message. The two oldest had always been the strong, reliable types. They were always willing to help family out, especially if it involved anything physical. Growing up, they were the ones Zara could always count on to help with moving things or assembling furniture, and now, she was glad to have them for this chaotic move.

It wasn't long before Janelle responded again: "They'll take care of it. We've got this."

Zara sighed in relief. At least that was one less thing to worry about. Between her aunts organizing and her cousins doing the heavy lifting, the move was already shaping up to be manageable. The only thing left was to make sure Niyah stayed on track. She could already imagine her fashionable aunt showing up late with her nails perfectly done, handing out advice on interior decor rather than carrying boxes.

With the plans in motion, Zara felt the weight of the upcoming move ease just a little. It wasn't just the physical work that her family would help with, but the emotional support too. Having them there would make it feel less like a burden and more like a family event. The thought of shared laughter and familiar faces made the whole process seem more manageable, even exciting. For once, the chaos of change felt like something she could embrace, surrounded by people who truly understood her.

Zara's phone buzzed again as she was packing up another box. This time, the message from her aunt made her laugh.

"I'm bringing Ellis, too. He can help with the light stuff."

Zara smiled, imagining her youngest cousin trying to keep up with his older brothers. Ellis was Janelle's youngest son, and though he was only 13, he was always eager to be included in anything his older brothers did. Zara could picture him trying to carry boxes half his size, wanting to feel just as important as his two oldest brothers.

She quickly typed back: "Perfect! We'll find plenty of light things for him to carry. Don't want him getting too tired!"

"We've got the heavy and the light covered," she responded. "We're glad you're moving back to Crest Ridge."

"Me too, auntie. Now y'all will be bothered with me every day."

"Not me. I know how to mute you." Niyah messaged.

Crest Ridge, the town where Zara and her family lived, was one of those picturesque southern cities known for its rich history and well-preserved architecture. The city was a perfect blend of old-world elegance and modern convenience. It was known as the kind of place where everyone knew each other, and weekends were spent outside, walking through tree-lined streets or gathering at the local diner.

The city had a strong reputation for fostering small businesses and nurturing entrepreneurs. The city's downtown area was dotted with quaint shops and family-owned establishments that had been passed down through generations. The streets were alive with the vibrant energy of local artisans, restaurateurs, and shop owners, all contributing to the town's unique character. Zara always appreciated the beauty of her hometown. From the sweet scent of fresh-cut grass to the view of the sprawling hills, it had always felt like home.

It was no wonder she decided to move back. After her mom passed, all Zara wanted to do was be by her family. She needed the comfort of familiar faces, the strength of her roots. The move was coming up fast, and there was still so much to do. At least with Janelle bringing all three of her children, Zara felt like she could take a breath. This was more than just a physical relocation; it was a step toward rebuilding a life she'd almost lost, one where her family would help her hold it all together again.

Zara's phone buzzed again, this time with a message from Niyah. "By the way, I'm bringing some of my famous banana pudding. You know you can't move without dessert!"

Zara laughed, imagining her aunt's impish grin. Niyah always found a way to make the most ordinary events feel special, and her banana pudding was a family favorite. It was a small gesture, but it was one that made Zara feel even more connected to her roots, as if the chaos of moving was just another excuse for a family gathering.

"You're a lifesaver, Auntie," Zara typed back, feeling a little lighter. "I'll save you a spot in the kitchen for it."

As she set her phone down, Zara took a deep breath, letting the familiar sounds of her family's messages wash over her. This move might be overwhelming, but with Janelle's organization, Niyah's humor, and the support of everyone else, it didn't feel so daunting. In fact, it was starting to feel like something she could actually look forward to—like a new chapter, filled with the love and laughter that had always defined her family.

Chapter 2

It was Saturday morning, and Zara's family had gathered to help her with the big move. The new apartment building was tucked into a quiet part of Crest Ridge, surrounded by trees that shaded the sidewalks. The only downside? The apartment was on the third floor. As if moving boxes wasn't exhausting enough, the steep stairs promised to make the process feel even longer. Still, Zara knew with her family by her side, they'd tackle the challenge together—one trip at a time.

Zara stood at the base of the staircase, hands on her hips, watching her two cousins haul boxes and furniture up the steep flights of stairs. She could hear Ellis somewhere nearby, probably chatting with his mom as they organized the lighter items. The cool morning air was already giving way to a warmer breeze, making the task even more tiring.

Zara's phone buzzed in her pocket. She pulled it out to see a message from her cousin Myia, who had stayed back for now but planned to come by later.

"Let me know if you need a break or some backup," the text read, followed by a string of laughing emojis. Zara smiled, feeling the familiar comfort of Myia's supportive, laid-back nature, knowing that when she did arrive, she'd bring a sense of calm to the chaos.

"But for real I gotta take Tyson to work since he couldn't find a ride. We'll come by later to help."

As she tucked her phone back into her pocket, Marcus appeared at the bottom of the stairs, slightly out of breath, giving her a playful look. "Third-floor apartment, Zara? Really? You're lucky we love you."

Zara laughed. "Trust me, I'll owe you big time after this."

"Don't forget about me either," Jordan said running up to them. "He's not the only one doing the heavy lifting."

"Lol I won't forget about you either. "

As the morning wore on and the family continued to lug boxes and furniture up the three floors, Niyah kept checking her phone. She had already decided that Malik would meet her after everything was done. There was no way she wanted the family to meet him just yet, especially with how overprotective they could be.

She typed out a quick message to Malik:

"Hey, I'm sending you the address. Wait until we finish, then we can meet up."

She hit send and took a deep breath, glancing around at Janelle and the others, who were busy getting Zara settled. She knew it would raise a million questions if her sisters or the kids got wind of Malik showing up. It was better this way—no drama, no explanations. Just a quiet meeting after the dust settled from the move. She'd introduce him when the time was right, but today wasn't that day.

Janelle, carrying a box of kitchen supplies, glanced over at her sister, who was standing off to the side, typing away on her phone. With a knowing smile, she raised an eyebrow and called out, "Well, well, look who's all mysterious today! Who's got you glued to your phone?"

Niyah quickly locked her screen, tucking the phone into her pocket and forcing a casual grin. "Just handling a few things, nothing major."

She smirked, clearly unconvinced. "Uh-huh, sure. You're acting shady. You got a secret boyfriend or something?"

"Please. I'm just staying on top of things. You know how it is."

"Uh-huh, you can't fool me. You're all smiley over there. If it's nothing, then show me the phone."

"Nope, not today! You'll find out soon enough."

She gave her sister a playful side eye, but with everything going on, she didn't push further. "Alright, keep your secrets for now, but I'll be waiting." She winked before heading back upstairs to help with the next load. Niyah let out a relieved sigh, thankful her sister didn't press her. She wasn't ready for anyone to know about Malik yet, especially not today.

They were in the middle of unpacking, boxes scattered everywhere, when a sharp knock echoed through the apartment. Everyone paused, and Zara, nearest to the door, sighed. "I'll get it."

She opened the door to reveal a woman standing there, arms crossed and an annoyed expression on her face. "Hi, I'm your downstairs neighbor," she began, her voice tight with frustration. "I don't know what you all are doing up here, but the noise has been nonstop. It's way too loud, and some of us are trying to enjoy our Saturday."

Before Zara could respond, Niyah stepped in, leaning against the door frame with a smirk. "We're moving in. It's not exactly a quiet activity, you know?"

The woman scowled. "Well, maybe you could keep it down a little. Some of us live here and don't appreciate the constant thumping around."

"Lady, it's a move. It'll be done when it's done. Why don't you get a life and chill for a few hours? You'll survive."

The neighbor's mouth dropped open in shock. "Excuse me?"

Zara, sensing things might escalate, quickly stepped between them. "We're almost done, really. We'll try to keep it down."

The neighbor huffed, her eyes narrowing at Niyah before she turned and stomped back down the stairs. As the door clicked shut, Niyah crossed her arms, shaking her head. "People really need to learn how to mind their own business."

Zara looked at her with a mix of amusement and exasperation. "Well, that's one way to meet the neighbors."

Janelle walked over, wiping her hands on a towel. "What did I miss?"

Zara just laughed. "Auntie's already making friends."

"Well since we're almost finished, who's ordering the pizzas? Remember to order mine as a veggie." Marcus yelled from the bedroom, "We know ma, we know. But you're welcome to come back to the meat side anytime you want." Ellis burst out laughing from the kitchen.

The unpacking continued as the morning stretched into the afternoon. Boxes were slowly but surely disappearing as Zara's things found their places in the new apartment. The two brothers, despite the grumbling about the stairs, were making quick work of the heavier items. Ellis helped his mom with lighter tasks, making sure everything was organized, while Niyah stayed on her phone, checking in now and then.

Once the food arrived, everyone was ready for a break. All the kids sat together at the kitchen table. Janelle, Niyah and Zara sat in a circle on the floor. Zara's stomach growled at the smell of pizza wafting through the hallway as the delivery guy knocked on the door.

"Finally," Jordan said, wiping sweat from his forehead as he dropped onto the nearest chair. "I was starting to think we'd never eat."

Zara grabbed the food and brought it inside, laying it out on the small kitchen counter. "Alright, let's take a break, everyone. You've all earned it. And before I forget, there's banana pudding in the refrigerator."

"Not for long," Jordan said. "You should have led with that!"

They gathered around, the boxes of pizza a welcome sight after a long morning of work. As they dug in, laughter and conversation filled the room. The tension from earlier with the neighbor faded away for the moment.

Marcus nudged Ellis with his elbow as they ate. "I bet Auntie's texting that secret boyfriend of hers. What do you think?" Ellis grinned but didn't say anything. "I can hear you, you know," Niyah said with a smirk.

Janelle smiled at the playful banter, but she couldn't shake the feeling that something was up with her sister. She decided to let it slide for now. After all, there were boxes to unpack and a house to settle into.

As they continued eating, Ellis, with a mischievous grin, chimed in, "Maybe Auntie's just texting the pizza guy. She's making sure we got enough pepperoni."

The table erupted in laughter, and even Niyah couldn't help but chuckle. She playfully tossed a napkin at Ellis. "You wish, little man. I'd never trust a pizza guy with my secrets." Ellis grinned, dodging the napkin and leaning back in his chair. "Oh, come on, auntie. I'm pretty sure he knows more than you think. The way you order your extra cheese is practically a confession." She laughed, raising her hands in mock surrender, "Alright, alright. But I'll never admit it."

With the mood lightened, the group settled into a more relaxed rhythm, their focus momentarily shifting from the exhausting move to enjoying a break and each other's company. Conversations flowed easily, ranging from fond childhood memories to casual plans for the week ahead. The clinking of glasses and the sound of contented sighs filled the room, and for a brief moment, it felt less like a move and more like a celebration of togetherness. Even the boxes stacked in every corner seemed less daunting as they shared this quiet, simple pleasure.

"So, what's the plan for tonight everyone?" Zara asked after they were finished. "Let's have a housewarming party." Niyah who couldn't stop smiling from looking at her phone said "Can't hang out tonight. I got a date with a guy I met online." Everyone stopped and looked at her. All types of questions were being asked but she tried to deflect them all. "Tell us about him. What is his name? What does he do? How long have you known him? Why haven't we met him?"

She just laughed and said "Gimme a moment. Y'all asked a lot of questions and all I will say is that he's a general manager at the gas station and he just moved down here last month after his divorce. I met him on a dating app and he's picking me up from here later."

Turning to Zara, she continued in a reassuring voice, "I only told him the apartment building, not your apartment number. He's going to meet me in the parking lot. He will text me when he arrives. As a matter of fact, I need to go change. I am not going out in this," she said as she grabbed a plastic bag of clothes and went to the bathroom to change. While she was changing, Myia and Tyson strolled in. Myia looked around at the half-eaten pizza boxes and raised an eyebrow. "Y'all started without us? Where's our food?"

Tyson, his stomach clearly growling, added, "Yeah, we're starving!"

Without missing a beat, Marcus leaned back in his chair, a sly grin spreading across his face. "Oh, the food? Yeah, it's right where you left it... in the car. You didn't bring to help us move all morning."

The room burst into laughter, and Myia shot him a playful glare. "Wow, really? You're gonna do us like that?"

He shrugged, still smirking. "Hey, pizza doesn't move itself. You snooze, you lose."

Janelle shook her head, chuckling as she slid a couple of untouched slices toward Myia and Tyson. "Don't mind him. There's plenty left. Help yourselves before he gets any more ideas."

Myia gave her cousin a playful nudge as she grabbed her slice, and Tyson dug in, relieved to finally eat. "Next time, I'll make sure we're here first," he said with a grin.

"Where's our mom?"

Janelle, leaning against the counter, gave a knowing smile. "Oh, your mom's busy getting ready for a date."

Myia's eyes widened, nearly dropping her pizza. "A date? With who?"

Janelle shrugged, feigning innocence. "You tell me. She's been glued to her phone all morning, texting someone. We don't know his name, though, and she's being all secretive about it."

Myia shook her head, both surprised and amused. "Unbelievable. First pizza, now I'm finding out my mom's out here dating like she's 25 again. The world's gone mad."

Janelle laughed, taking a sip of her drink. "Oh, don't worry. She'll be out soon enough, and you can interrogate her yourself."

While they continued to catch up and break down the boxes, outside the apartment building, the hum of the day was suddenly interrupted by the deep rumble of a car engine. A tan SUV pulled up to the curb, its bass thumping so loudly that the windows in Zara's new apartment rattled slightly. Heads turned toward the window, the loud music grabbing everyone's attention. Marcus raised an eyebrow and peered outside. "Who rolls up like that in the middle of the day?" he muttered, stepping closer to get a better look.

The SUV sat there for a moment, the driver's side door still closed, music blaring through the open windows. Janelle frowned, crossing her arms. "I hope that's not one of Zara's new neighbors. This place is gonna be fun if it is." She glanced at Zara, raising an eyebrow. "You sure you're ready for this?" Zara shrugged, trying to keep her tone light. "I guess it's all part of the adventure. But yeah, a little peace would be nice." As the music pulsed, the bass rattling the windows, Janelle sighed. "Well, if nothing else, it'll keep things interesting."

Chapter 3

Myia joined Marcus by the window and squinted down at the vehicle. "Looks familiar, doesn't it?" she said, trying to place where she had seen the SUV before. He leaned in, his brow furrowing. "Wait... is that the same car that was parked outside the coffee shop last week?" Myia nodded slowly, her curiosity piqued. "I think so. But why would they be here?" Tyson shrugged, uninterested in the commotion. "I don't know, but whoever it is, they really need to chill with that music." He gestured toward the window, clearly annoyed by the constant bass thumping.

Jordan turned to look at the bathroom door. "It could be her ride," he said with a smirk, half-joking but with a hint of suspicion.

Janelle glanced toward the door too. "Wouldn't be surprised. She's been acting all secretive today."

Before anyone could say anything else, the music abruptly cut off, and the SUV's engine went silent. The car had a custom paint job that looked like it was bathed in a golden glow. The vehicle was a visual masterpiece, with a sleek tan exterior that shimmered thanks to its glossy, shiny coat finish. The darkness of tinted glass obscured the interior, while the black rims, with their bold, angular design, added a sharp contrast. It eventually parked at the curb. The car's windows, partially rolled down, seemed to vibrate with every pulse of the beat, causing the balcony windows to quiver.

Seated in the driver's seat was Malik Johnson. He was an African American man in his late forties. His deep mahogany complexion glowed with a natural radiance, complemented by his salt-and-pepper goatee, which was meticulously groomed. His strong jawline and well-defined cheekbones gave him an authoritative yet approachable look. His eyes, sharp and expressive, were framed by a slight, knowing smile, suggesting both wisdom and warmth. His short haircut was impeccably groomed, with every line and fade perfectly maintained. The sunlight caught the subtle glint of his diamond grill, which was a prominent feature of his smile. As he sat in the car, he bobbed his head to the beat, his hands gripping the steering wheel with a relaxed intensity. Malik was lost in the music, his head nodding in sync with the unwavering beat.

Niyah emerged from the bathroom, pausing to glance at her reflection in a nearby mirror. She had on an animal print shirt, its vibrant leopard and zebra patterns cascading in shades of gold and black. The shirt hugged her in all the right places while the sheer sleeves showed off her upper arm tattoos. The neckline was just low enough to be sophisticated yet alluring, striking a balance that showcased her taste without being overpowering. Her ripped black pants revealed just the right amount of skin to add interest while also emphasizing her curves in all the right places. Her shoes, a bold wild animal pattern, matched the same daring design as her shirt, creating an effortlessly coordinated look. The outfit was completed with a small black purse that hung casually from her shoulder, adding a touch of sleekness to her edgy, yet refined style.

"Y'all are really up in my business, huh?" she said, catching the tail end of the conversation, her tone playful but with a hint of warning. "I heard everything."

Myia raised an eyebrow, grinning. "Oh, so it's true. You're really out here getting all dolled up for a date while the rest of us break our backs moving boxes?"

Niyah smirked, smoothing down her clothes. "The only ones that were breaking their backs had pizza and pudding. Besides, I never said I'd be here for the whole move. Gotta have some fun too."

"Who's the guy, Mom?" Tyson chimed in, still chewing on his pizza. "Does he know what he's getting into?"

She rolled her eyes dramatically. "His name is Malik. And yes, he's fully aware of what he's getting into, thank you very much."

Janelle shook her head, smiling. "You better be careful, sis. At least let one of us meet him for your protection. You're the only sister I got left."

"Stop worrying . You're beginning to sound like our mom. It's just a first date. I'll introduce him later when the time is right." While they were talking, Marcus went out to the balcony to take a picture of the SUV.

"These kids are like detectives, they won't stop until they get all the background on him. You know this..."

"Oh, I'm sure," Niyah replied with a grin, tossing a playful glance around the room. "But I'm keeping this one under wraps for now. Gotta keep you all on your toes." She winked, savoring the mystery, knowing full well her family would be buzzing with curiosity long after the conversation shifted.

Jordan leaned back, a mischievous glint in his eyes. "Don't worry, Auntie. We'll meet him eventually... one way or another."

The room filled with laughter again, but Myia just shook her head. "Well, have fun on your little mystery date. But don't think you're off the hook. We'll be asking questions when you get back."

Niyah winked. "I wouldn't expect anything less." She grabbed her purse and, with a final glance in the mirror, made her way to the door, leaving the rest of the family shaking their heads with smiles on their faces.

An hour later, Janelle told them she was getting ready to go home. She had been feeling worse for the past few hours but didn't want to say anything to take away from the mini family reunion. The last time they were all together like this had been at their older sister Felicia's, Zara's mom, funeral five years ago. Everyone was busy with their schedules, so today just felt like the old days—easy, comfortable, and filled with laughter. Walking downstairs, the cousins chatted amiably, still telling jokes as usual, their voices echoing with warmth in the dimming light. Despite the years and the grief they had all shared, today felt like a small, welcome reprieve, a reminder of the bond they still had.

Outside, the evening air had a crispness to it, signaling the coming of summer. The stars were just starting to appear, and the streetlights cast soft, yellow pools of light onto the sidewalk. Janelle paused for a moment, looking out at the apartment building. It was quiet and peaceful. The world seemed to have slowed down for a moment, offering her a rare chance to just breathe.

Before she got into her car, she sent a quick message to Niyah.

"It was great catching up with you today. Love you, sis. Hope we can all do this again soon."

As she started the engine, the hum of the car felt almost comforting. She didn't know how long it would take before the weight of everything—the move, the years that had passed, the moments that had slipped away—settled back in, but for now, she was content. The laughter, the teasing, the familiar faces, those were the things that had always anchored her, and for today, they were enough.

As Janelle pulled away from the building, she couldn't help but glance in the rearview mirror. The streetlight flickered in the distance, casting a warm glow on the gathering that was still going on outside. It was almost surreal to think about how much time had passed since they'd all been together like this. Five years felt like a lifetime, and yet, the laughter and the familiar banter had made it feel like no time had passed at all. Her phone buzzed in the mount on the dashboard. Quickly glancing at the screen, she saw a message from Zara.

"Love you, Auntie. Take care of yourself, okay? We'll talk soon."

Janelle smiled, feeling a surge of affection for her niece. Zara was the reason they had all come back together today. She had moved back to Crest Ridge, and it felt like a new chapter in their lives. Janelle hadn't realized how much she'd missed her niece until they were all sitting around the table, talking about old times. She quickly typed a response:

"Love you too sweetie. Welcome back!"

After sending the message, she returned her focus to driving. Her thoughts kept drifting back to her sister, Felicia. It still hurt. The pain was always there, lingering just beneath the surface. But today had been different. Being with family, hearing their jokes and their stories, it had softened the edges of that grief. She could almost hear Felicia's voice, laughing along with the rest of them.

Janelle made a mental note to check in on her health more often. She had been feeling off for a while, but she didn't want to worry anyone. She had always been the strong one, the one who held everything together. But sometimes, even the strongest among them needed to lean on someone else. else. It was hard to admit, but she couldn't keep up the facade forever. She made a decision to go ahead and make an appointment before things got worse. She sighed deeply, not sure what tomorrow would bring but grateful for today. For now, she would hold on to the memories of the evening, knowing that the warmth of family was a constant she could always return to.

Chapter 4

Niyah hadn't been on what she calls a real date in a long time. She was anticipating not hearing the words "mom or grandma" for a couple of hours. Plus, she felt extremely comfortable with Malik since she wasn't feeling any bad vibes. They had been chatting online for a few weeks, and their conversations had a natural flow. They bonded over their mutual love for old school west coast rap music and horror movies. She knew she made the right decision by meeting in person. She started to relax a little as they drove away, enjoying the simplicity of just being in the moment.

"So, what are the plans for tonight?" she asked over the music, turning toward him with a playful glance.

He grinned, eyes on the road. "My homeboy is throwing a party tonight. I figured we'd stop by, grab something to eat afterward, or catch a late movie."

She smiled, liking the sound of that. It felt easy, not rushed, and she was looking forward to a night without expectations. She settled back in her seat, the music filling the space between them as the city lights flickered outside the window. The soft hum of the car blended with the rhythm of the song, creating a quiet, comforting atmosphere. For the first time in weeks, she felt like she could just be, without worrying about what came next.

She began to start rapping to the music as she watched the streetlights pass them by. They also had some good conversations along the way about the local high school football rivalry. It was the end of school season, so they passed by a lot of school decorations and yard signs saying, "My Graduate lives here.' While talking they found out that they may have crossed paths when they were younger since they went to rival schools.

The party was held at an old barn off a dirt road in the country, which was in the next county. The venue was so far off the road that if someone was driving on that road, they would miss it. Niyah noticed a lot of action when they turned in. She saw so many cars there, she didn't think there was a spot for them to park. Luck would have it that Malik was able to find a spot at the front, right next to a row of tall, weathered fences that framed the barn. As they stepped out of the car, the faint sounds of music and laughter drifted toward them, mingling with the crisp, earthy scent of the surrounding fields. The place was alive with energy, and despite the crowded parking lot, Niyah couldn't help but think that this was exactly the kind of party she'd envisioned.

"Wow, it looks like they've really gone all out for this party," she said looking at all the vehicles. "It's a lot of cars here. They must have invited everyone they knew."

"Yeah, I'm impressed. I was expecting something a bit more low-key, but this is fantastic."

"I just hope I don't end up surrounded by people I don't know. I thought you said this would be like a small party."

"My homie said it was. But don't worry. I've got your back. We'll stick together, and if you start to feel uncomfortable, let me know."

"Okay. I'll give you a sign."

Malik smiled and said "Let's head in so I can make a quick appearance. Then we can get something to eat"

They started walking towards the door when Niyah's eye caught a small table with a sign reading "Entry Fee: $10" and a man in casual attire is standing behind it, collecting fees. She quickly followed as her date walked past and into the building. As they stepped through the large, wooden barn doors, they were instantly transported to a time when they didn't have a care in the world. The energy was mesmerizing and contagious.

The barn, usually a humble, rustic space, had been transformed into a vibrant dance hall for the evening. The room was a kaleidoscope of bright neon lights that danced in sync with the beats. The walls were adorned with streamers and glitter decorations in hold hues. A large, glittering disco ball hung from the ceiling in the middle of the room casting playful lights. It was just the added touch needed.

As they went further into the room, she realized neither she nor Malik was dressed for the party. It made her a little sad because she would have loved to show off her style, especially in a setting like this where everyone else seemed to have put in the effort. But she remembered it was their first date, so obviously this stop wasn't planned. She just hoped that she would have some fun while they were there, even if it meant blending in with the crowd instead of standing out. Still, as the music thumped and the warmth of conversation filled the air, she couldn't help but feel a little more at ease, knowing Malik was by her side.

There was an area on the right side for food and drinks. The first two tables were the punch bowls. There were a couple of people standing around the bowls who were dressed in high-waisted denim, chunky sneakers, and graphic tees. One of them sported a vintage FUBU jacket with bold, graffiti-like tags, while another rocked a pair of shiny, gold chain necklaces that clinked together with every exaggerated gesture as he told a story on how long it took for him to find the right pieces. The next few tables had a large variety of different foods and snacks, including meatballs, wings, pizza rolls, Dunkaroos, and cheesy nachos. And at the far end were the drinks tables.

These tables had wine coolers, both alcoholic and nonalcoholic, cocktails, and she swore she saw someone pouring from Boone's Farm. She couldn't believe that there was a variety of Boone's Farm and Alize. Directly across from that area was a lounge area with plush seating and low tables, providing a comfortable spot for guests to take a break from the dance floor.

To the far right was the deejay's area surrounded by big speakers. In the center of the room was the dance floor. The dance floor itself was a captivating sight. It was adorned with intricate patterns and bold colors that would make even an introvert want to join in the fun. People are already moving to the rhythm, their steps synchronized with the beat of the music. The energy was infectious, and one couldn't help but be drawn into the collective vibe of the room.

Before she could take the room in entirely, she saw someone coming their way wearing a gold chain and a "Fresh Prince" jersey with sleeve tattoos on both arms peeking out underneath. "Hey man, glad you made it! And who's this lovely lady?"

"Hey Tony, this is Niyah, the one that I've been telling you about" he said. Tony was taller than Malik by a couple of inches and his build was more toned than muscular. If she had a guess, it would have been from a basketball court. His caramel toned face was framed by a thick, well-maintained beard and he was wearing a pair of Dwayne Wayne glasses.

"Ma'am, you are one beautiful lady." Tony said as he grabbed her hand, giving one of his playful smiles showing two deep dimples. "Too bad you're taken, otherwise I'll swoop you up."

"Nice to meet you. I'm sure you have a lot of ladies that you could be asking out."

Malik didn't like how his friend was treating his date. He knew Tony was a big flirt with the ladies, but he didn't think he would do it on his date. He cleared his throat and said "Can you keep yourself busy while we catch up? I promise that we won't be long?" She watched them as they walked away, thinking they looked more like brothers instead of friends.

As they walked away, Niyah ventured towards the center of the dance floor. She noticed some people were gathered around what appeared to be an impromptu dance battle. In the center of the circle, two dancers are going head-to-head. One is dressed in a bright, geometric-patterned hoodie and baggy pants, executing smooth, fluid moves that blend break dancing with sharp, precise footwork. The other, sporting a classic bomber jacket and a pair of retro joggers, counters with a series of popping and locking moves that make the crowd erupt in cheers.

The music changed to another song and the crowd dispersed. But she was still in a hyper mood, so she started to dance. As her movements became more energetic, the people near her noticed. It was almost like they were drawn to her. When the next song played, more people gathered around and even joined in with her. With each passing moment, she becomes more absorbed in the music, her body moving with an almost instinctive grace.

She was feeling more at eased. She knew Malik went to talk to his friend, so she felt safe in the middle of the crowd. She knew nothing to happen to her if she was surrounded by others in public. The DJ notices the crowd's enthusiasm and cranks up the music even more, adding to the excitement.

Not everyone was feeling the same way. Malik was done talking to Tony and was watching Niyah from across the room. His smile faded as he watched her dancing with some people that he didn't even know. He was getting more heated the more he continued to watch the attention fall on her. He was trying to calm his nerves, but he didn't like the way they were dancing so close. He didn't like that at all. Their date tonight was to get to know each other, but he was getting the feeling that it was slipping away.

He stopped by the bar to get a drink for him and her. His grip on the drinks got tighter the more he looked at Niyah and the men around her. He was getting frustrated but since they were in public, he wanted to keep his composure. As he approached the group, he noticed a few men lingering nearby clearly watching her movements. One of them, a well-dressed older gentleman, seemed like he was ready to make a move on her.

"I was watching you from across the room and I thought you may be thirsty from the dancing, so I brought you a drink." He said as he proceeded to give her the drink.

Niyah, trying not to look embarrassed, replied "I appreciate it, but I would prefer to get my own drink or at least watch the bartender pour it himself."

"Are you saying that you don't trust me. You think that I would slip something in your drink that fast? The bar is right there." He replied loudly.

Niyah trying to stay calm, "Umm you're causing a scene for no reason. I'm just vibing to the music."

" Oh, so I'm causing a scene now? Well if you weren't such a freaking flirt, everyone wouldn't be looking at you right now."

"Really? A flirt? If you were here with me instead of leaving me alone while you talk to your friend, then we wouldn't have this conversation right now."

They didn't notice that the music stopped playing and everyone in the room was staring at them. Malik knew he had to say something to get all the eyes away. He really liked her, but he knew he had some jealous tendencies that he needed to work on. Maybe this was a test, maybe not. Even so, he didn't want to cause a scene at the party, and he didn't want to go viral with someone in the crowd recording him.

Niyah's excitement had dimmed, and her patience was wearing thin. When they agreed to meet in person, this wasn't what she had imagined. Malik's behavior was unexpected. She tried to ignore it at first, but causing a scene made it harder to overlook.

"Look, I apologize if I gave you the wrong impression," he started. "I'm not normally like this. Especially when I'm in the presence of someone who's as fun and beautiful as you. Let me make it up to you."

Chapter 5

She stared at him for a moment, weighing her options. A part of her wanted to tell him to forget it, but another part of her wanted to give him a chance. Maybe dinner could turn the night around. "I don't know," Niyah sighed. "Your energy has been off tonight, and now you want to make it up?"

"I was just... distracted. I know I was off," he admitted, rubbing the back of his neck. "But I'm here now. Just tell me what you want to do."

"Alright," she said, her voice cool but not entirely closed off. "There's a spot that I've been wanting to try, The Crimson Manor . It's not far from here. We can eat there."

Malik knew the place. It was classy, a little upscale. It seemed like her way of giving him one more chance to salvage the night. "The Crimson Manor it is. I promise, I'll make this better."

When they arrived at the restaurant, Malik's heart sank a little. The parking lot was packed, with barely a space left. The restaurant's warm lights glowed through the large front windows, and inside, they could see people chatting and enjoying their meals. It was clearly a busy night. Malik glanced at Niyah, unsure if she'd mind the crowd. But her smile remained, unfazed by the hustle. "Looks like we're not the only ones with a craving tonight," she said, her voice light. Malik chuckled, feeling a little better. "Yeah, looks like it. But hey, we'll make it work." As they found a spot near the back, he hoped the wait wouldn't be too long. He'd been looking forward to this date all week.

As they walked up to the entrance, Malik glanced at Niyah. She still seemed a bit distant, and he hoped that bringing her there would help ease the tension. The hostess, a young woman with a friendly smile, greeted them. "Welcome to The Crimson Manor! How many are in your party?"

Malik, realizing now that he probably should have called ahead, "Just the two of us."

"Great! For a table of two, there's about a 15 to 20 minute wait. Is that okay?"

Malik looked over at Niyah, worried that the delay might push her patience too far. She raised an eyebrow but didn't seem too upset. "Yeah, that's fine," she said with a shrug, still scrolling through her phone.

"Alright, we'll call you when your table's ready," the hostess smiled as she handed Malik a small pager.

They moved to the side of the waiting area, and Malik sighed internally. He was already on thin ice, and now they had to wait. But he was determined to stay calm. He needed to turn this night around. He tried to strike up some light conversation, hoping to bring her back to the Niyah he'd been texting all this time.

Thirty minutes later, they followed the hostess past a vibrant bar area to a cozy booth that bathed in the soft, amber light of the restaurant. They were given menus, but Niyah already knew what she wanted. She looked at the menu online on the way there. Malik was surprised because he thought he would have to suggest the specials to her or lead her to what he thought was the best thing on the menu. She immediately returned the menu and ordered.

As the evening progressed, Niyah found herself feeling a bit more at ease. Sitting across from Malik at their table, she took a sip of her drink and exhaled, letting go of the lingering tension from earlier. Despite the rocky start, she decided she didn't want to let it overshadow their time together. She had taken a chance on him, believing there was something worth exploring. Their conversations online had been engaging, with moments of laughter and vulnerability that made her feel like she was getting to know the real him.

Malik nervously cut into his steak, his hands a little shaky as he tried to steady himself. "I've been meaning to apologize for the earlier part of the evening." His eyes were steady, his voice genuine. "I guess I got caught up in my own head and acted like an idiot."

Niyah looked at him, trying to gauge his sincerity. She didn't want to rush to forgiveness, but there was something in his expression that made her soften a bit. "No one's perfect, and I'm glad we had a chance to clear the air." Malik continued, "I just felt like I wasn't fully present. I was overthinking everything and didn't want to mess things up with you. I'm sorry if I came off weird or jealous."

Her lips curved into a small smile, reassured by his honesty. "Thank you for recognizing your behavior," she said, her voice calm. "I was bothered by it earlier, to be honest. I accept your apology."

Malik looked relieved, a hint of a grin forming as he picked up his fork again. "Good. I just wanted to clear the air before I ruin this meal." Niyah chuckled softly, feeling the tension slip away. "Well, you've got nothing to worry about now," she said. "Let's enjoy the meal."

The two continued talking animatedly over their dinner. The conversation had flowed effortlessly from one topic to another, covering everything from their bucket lists to their most embarrassing stories. "*This makes up for earlier*," she thought. "*I'm feeling a lot better about him.*" Malik leaned in, trying to contain himself from laughing. "So, you mean to tell me that you took an edible after smoking? That sounds brave."

She laughed; her eyes sparkling. "Yep, it took too long for the weed to kick in. Trust me, I learned my lesson. Never again." Malik laughed. "I bet you won't. I haven't tried either one, but I hope you don't hold that against me."

They were still laughing at Malik's stories when the waitress arrived to clear their plates. Niyah glanced at her phone and saw the time. It was much later than she'd realized. Her smile faded and was replaced by a look of surprise. Malik noticed immediately, the shift in her expression making him tense up slightly.

"Time really flew by, didn't it?" he said, trying to keep the atmosphere light. "I've had a fun time tonight."

Niyah shook her head, almost as if clearing her thoughts. "I agree," she replied, her voice softer now. "I just didn't realize it was getting so late."

Malik could sense her apprehension and hurried to reassure her. "I'm really glad we did this," he said, leaning forward. "I know things started off rough, but it's been a good night, right?"

She looked up at him, seeing the hint of nervousness in his eyes. Despite everything, he seemed genuine. She couldn't deny that she'd enjoyed herself, even after the initial awkwardness. He had redeemed the evening with his stories and jokes, and she could appreciate the effort he'd made to lighten the mood.

"Yeah, it has," she said, her smile returning briefly. "I didn't think I'd be out this late, though."

"I get it," he replied, nodding. "But hey, I appreciate you giving me another shot. I know I didn't make the best first impression."

"It's not all about first impressions," she said with a hint of amusement. "It's about how you finish."

Malik leaned back in his seat with a grin, trying to keep the mood light. "Speaking of finishing... does that mean you want to finish our date at my place?" His voice had a playful tone, but there was an underlying edge, almost testing the waters.

Niyah felt her shoulders tense at the suggestion. She smiled, trying to soften the rejection. "I appreciate the offer, Malik," she replied, choosing her words carefully, "but I'd prefer if you just took me home tonight."

Malik's grin faltered, his eyes narrowing just a fraction. For a moment, the smile on his face felt like a mask slipping. She noticed it,the brief shift in his expression, and felt a pang of discomfort. He quickly forced a smile back, but the change was unmistakable. That creeping sense of jealousy, the one she had caught glimpses of earlier in the evening, seemed to be making a return.

"Home, huh?" he said, his voice slightly tighter. "You're sure you don't want to come over, even for a little while?"

Niyah's instincts told her to tread carefully. "Yeah, I'm sure," she replied with a polite firmness. "It's getting late, and I've got a lot going on tomorrow. I just... want to take it slow, you know?"

Malik's fingers tapped against the table, a steady, almost impatient rhythm. He nodded, but she could see the muscle in his jaw clench, a telltale sign of his growing frustration. "I get it," he said, the edge in his voice now more noticeable. "But we've been talking for a while now. You've gotta trust me at some point, right?"

Niyah took a breath, maintaining eye contact to show she wasn't backing down. "It's not about trust, Malik. I just want to go home tonight."

Malik exhaled slowly, trying to reel in his emotions. He knew he was pushing, but he couldn't help the nagging feeling that she was pulling away. And that made him uneasy, more than he wanted to admit. "Alright," he finally said, forcing a smile that didn't quite reach his eyes. "I'll take you home."

"Thank you, Malik. I really appreciate it."

As they left the restaurant, the lightheartedness of earlier felt like it had evaporated into the cool night air. Niyah kept her gaze straight ahead, wondering if giving Malik a second chance had been a mistake. He, on the other hand, was struggling to keep his jealousy at bay as he led her to the car in silence.

Chapter 6

As they walked to the car, Malik tried to shake off his frustration. He opened the passenger door for Niyah, and she slid in with a polite Thank you. When he got in the driver's seat and started the car, he took a breath, seemingly to gather his thoughts. He had to change his tone and mood so it wouldn't raise any red flags.

The car hummed softly as it glided out the parking lot and onto the quiet streets, the city lights casting fleeting shadows on the dashboard. The faint scent of her perfume lingered in the air, mixing with the leather upholstery and the faint remnants of their dinner. Malik's eyes flicked to her once, her profile illuminated by the streetlights that passed them by in quick succession.

The silence between them had settled into an uncomfortable stillness. He knew Niyah had been resolute when she said she wanted to go home. He'd already tried to convince her once, maybe twice, but she hadn't budged. She wasn't the type to be swayed by charm or coaxing, and he respected that. But he wasn't ready to let the night end just yet.

Malik shifted in his seat, glancing at her again, trying to read her expression in the dim light. She was looking out the window now, her arms crossed lightly over her chest. Her profile was unreadable, but the set of her jaw told him she wasn't going to change her mind.

"You know," he began, carefully, "I was thinking... It's still pretty early. We could just go back to my place for a bit, watch a movie or something. I don't want the night to end just yet."

She turned her head to face him, her expression neutral but firm. "Malik," she said, her voice steady, "I really appreciate the invitation, but I'm set on going home. I'm babysitting my grandson tomorrow, and I need to rest." She began texting both her children that she was heading home so she didn't notice the expression on his face.

He exhaled slowly, taking another turn. "I'm not trying to push you, you know. I just..." He paused, trying to find the right words, the ones that wouldn't come off as pressure but would make her understand. "I just thought we were having a good time. And I thought that we could keep it going for a little longer."

A beat of silence passed. He could feel the frustration in the back of his throat, but he swallowed it down. This wasn't the time for stubbornness. He knew what he wanted, and he thought he knew what she wanted, too. It wasn't just about tonight; it was about the way they'd been circling each other for weeks, the tension building every time they were together. But she was always so cautious, always holding back. And tonight, it felt like one last test.

"No, Malik," she interrupted, her tone firmer now. She didn't want to hurt his feelings, but she needed to set a clear boundary. "It's not about you. I'm just not comfortable tonight, and I want to go home."

His forced smile faded, replaced by an annoyed frown. Malik pressed his lips together, his eyes darkening with a flicker of anger. Niyah saw it, but she didn't look away. She could tell he was fighting to keep his temper in check, but something told her it wouldn't last much longer. Her fingers curled into the fabric of her jeans, her nails digging into the material as her heart raced. She felt like a fool tonight. The signs were there and she completely ignored them. It was like he had two different personas, like Dr. Jekyll and Mr. Hyde, except now she was trapped in a moving vehicle and she had no idea what would happen next.

The car swerved slightly as Malik jerked his head to glance at her for a brief second, his eyes cold, devoid of any warmth. "You think you know everything, don't you?" he muttered, the words sharp and laced with venom. Her breath hitched, but she refused to back down. She met his gaze, her lips trembling but firm. The weight of his stare was heavy, suffocating, and she could almost hear the crackle of the tension in the air between them. Something had broken; she could feel it.

Suddenly, Malik let out a cold, bitter laugh. "You know," he said, his voice low and edged with anger, "I went through a lot of trouble to plan this night. I paid for dinner, waited for you at that party... It was supposed to be a good time. And now you want me to just drop you off like nothing happened?"

She stiffened, her heart racing. "Malik, I told you—"

"I heard what you said," he cut her off sharply, not taking his eyes off the road. "But what I'm saying is, you owe me. And you're gonna repay me, either one way or another."

Her blood ran cold. Niyah's mind raced as she tried to figure out what he meant. There was a cold edge to his words that hadn't been there before. He wasn't just trying to convince her; he was trying to control her.

"Malik, please," she said softly, trying to keep her voice steady. "Just take me home."

But Malik only laughed again, more bitterly this time. "Take you home? Nah, I think we're gonna talk about how this night ends, not you." His fingers tightened on the wheel, and she could see the anger in his eyes.

Panic set in. Niyah slowly reached for her phone in her pocket, her mind racing with thoughts of how to get out of the car. Her fingers trembled as she tried to press the unlock button, but Malik's eyes flicked to her movement, and his expression darkened.

"What are you doing?" he snapped, reaching over to grab her wrist with a bruising grip.

"I-I was just—"

"Don't lie to me!" he shouted, his voice shaking with anger. "I've been nice. I've been patient. But if you keep trying to play me, you're going to find out that I'm not the guy to mess with."

Tears began to well up in her eyes as she realized how quickly things had escalated. She was trapped in the car with a man who was losing his temper, and she didn't know what he might do next. She needed to find a way out and fast.

"Malik, please," she whispered, her voice trembling. "Just let me go home. We can talk about this later, okay?"

But he wasn't listening anymore. He was too caught up in his own anger, too focused on getting what he thought he deserved. And she was left wondering how she could get out of this situation before things got even worse. Niyah spoke, trying to stay calm. "If you need money, I can pay you back. We just need to find an ATM, and I'll get you what you want."

Malik glanced at her, his eyes narrowing with suspicion. "You think you can just buy your way out of this?" he scoffed. "I don't want your money. I want something else."

She felt the dread growing in the pit of her stomach. She was running out of options, and Malik wasn't making this easy. Her heart pounded as she glanced out the window, realizing that they had left the main streets behind. The familiar buildings and streetlights had disappeared, replaced by a dark, desolate neighborhood she didn't recognize.

"Where are we going?" she asked, her voice barely steady.

Malik didn't answer immediately, keeping his eyes fixed on the road ahead. He seemed to be deep in thought, wrestling with something in his mind. Finally, he muttered, "You said you'd pay me back, huh?"

"Yes," she replied quickly, trying to sound convincing. "Just... stop at an ATM, and I'll take out whatever you want."

But Malik wasn't budging. "You don't get it, do you?" he said, his tone cold and distant. "I've been used and played with before. I'm not letting that happen again. You're gonna pay me back one way or another."

Niyah's pulse raced, and her thoughts scrambled for a solution. She couldn't let this situation spiral further. She had to keep him talking, keep him thinking there was something to gain. She had to find a moment to escape, a way to get to safety. "Malik, listen to me," she pleaded, forcing her voice to stay calm. "If you just stop the car and let me go to the ATM, I can make this right. We can both just walk away, no harm done."

He laughed, a harsh and joyless sound that sent chills down her spine. "You still think you can talk your way out of this?" he sneered. "You must think I'm stupid." The streetlights were getting scarcer, and the road ahead seemed to lead deeper into the unfamiliar neighborhood. Niyah didn't recognize a single landmark, and she realized with growing horror that Malik was taking her somewhere isolated.

"Malik," she tried again, her voice trembling, "please, I don't know where we're going. Just—"

"Shut up!" he snapped. "You're gonna give me what I want. One way or another."

Chapter 7

Niyah knew then that talking wasn't going to work. She needed a new plan and fast. Desperately, she scanned the road ahead, searching for any sign of help or an opportunity to escape. Her mind was racing, fear and adrenaline battling within her as she tried to stay one step ahead. Her eyes darted to the side, catching sight of an abandoned gas station up ahead, its flickering sign offering a faint glimmer of hope. She knew it was a risk, but at this point, any chance to break free was worth the gamble.

Malik was driving deeper into the darkness, and she did not like where this was headed. Niyah checked her phone to see the battery percentage. She subtly glanced down at her phone, her fingers trembling as she unlocked the screen. The battery was at 12%. She felt a surge of panic, realizing she might not have much time to call for help. Her mind raced with the possibilities: Should she turn on her location and hope someone in her family saw it? Should she text someone? Should she call 911?

She fought to steady her breathing as he continued to drive, seemingly lost in his thoughts. Niyah didn't want to make any sudden movements that might set him off. She needed a plan, and she needed it now. Turning on her location could give her family a clue if something went wrong, but she feared Malik might notice and get angry.

As her finger hovered over the location-sharing button, she glanced at Malik out of the corner of her eye. He seemed unaware of her actions for now, but she didn't want to push her luck. *"Is this worth the risk?"* she thought. If she made the wrong move and he noticed, things could escalate quickly. But if she did nothing, who would know where she was?

Taking a deep breath, Niyah made a split-second decision. She turned on her location and prayed that someone might see it. "It's better than nothing," she thought. Then, she locked the phone and held it tightly in her lap, praying she made the right choice.

The seconds seemed to drag, each one stretching out, loaded with the weight of her decision. She kept her gaze fixed forward, her chest tightening with the uncertainty that gnawed at her insides. Malik didn't speak as he continued driving. She could feel the tension in the air between them, a charged silence that made every sound seem too loud. She fought the urge to look at him, to see if he'd noticed the flicker of movement on her phone. Her heartbeat pounded in her ears as she waited, holding her breath as though the slightest noise would shatter the fragile moment of secrecy she'd created.

Her phone remained locked in her lap, the small device now carrying the weight of her safety, her choice, and the secrets she had just taken a step closer to uncovering. She couldn't shake the feeling that, even though she had done something to protect herself, she was still walking a razor-thin line. One wrong move, one glance from Malik, and everything could change. But right now, all she could do was wait.

Suddenly, Malik's voice broke through the silence, startling her. "What are you doing over there?" he demanded, his tone suspicious. Niyah quickly shoved the phone into her pocket. "Just checking the time," she lied, forcing herself to sound calm. "It's late, Malik. I think it's best we just call it a night."

But Malik wasn't convinced. He shot her a sidelong glare. "I'm not stupid," he muttered. "I told you before that you're not walking away from this." Her heart pounded in her chest, the words sinking into her like a cold weight. She forced herself to breathe, her mind scrambling for a way out, but Malik's voice cut through her thoughts again, harsh and low. "Don't even think about it."

Malik's car bumped along a rough, unpaved road, the tires kicking up small rocks as he turned into a back entrance of a park. Her stomach churned with a mix of fear and confusion. There were no streetlights, just the dim glow of the car's headlights slicing through the dark trees that loomed over them. Niyah glanced out of the window, recognizing nothing. Her pulse quickened, the silence of the park pressing in on her. "Where are we?" she asked, trying to keep the fear out of her voice.

Malik didn't respond right away, his face shadowed and unreadable. Finally, he muttered, "A quiet place. You said you needed to stop at an ATM, right?" His voice was laced with sarcasm, making it clear he didn't believe her excuse. She could feel the underlying threat in his words, the way he seemed to be daring her to try something.

The car came to a stop near a dense line of trees. He put it in park but left the engine running, the headlights still illuminating the empty path ahead of them. He turned to face her, his eyes narrowed, the silence between them thick and unnerving. She could feel the weight of his gaze pressing down on her. Her hands trembled in her lap, but she kept her chin lifted, refusing to show any fear. The darkness outside seemed to close in around them, the night swallowing up any sense of escape.

Niyah knew she needed to act, but she couldn't think straight. Her hands shook as she fumbled with her seat belt, trying to come up with something to say or do to diffuse the situation. She had to keep him calm, at least until she could figure out a way out of this."I..I'm sorry, Malik," she said, her voice trembling. " I overreacted earlier. I just... I need to get home, okay? Please, let's just go."

Malik leaned back in his seat, his fingers tapping rhythmically on the steering wheel. He studied her for what felt like an eternity, his expression unreadable. "I knew you were just like the others. " he said, his voice low. "All y'all women are just the same. Gold diggers. But I will say this, it will be the last time that a woman tries to play me!""

She swallowed hard, choosing her words carefully. "I just... I want to go home to my kids. That's all."

Malik shook his head slowly, his lips curving into a bitter smile. "You'll go home tonight" he said, his voice dropping to a dangerous whisper. "After I get what's owed."

Her pulse quickened at the threat in his voice. "What do you mean, 'what's owed'?" she asked, her voice shaking despite her best efforts to stay calm. Malik's smile widened, but there was no humor in it. It was just a cold, calculated malice that made her skin crawl. "You know exactly what I'm talking about," he replied, his tone low and menacing. "You owe me for tonight. You don't walk away from that."

Panic surged through Niyah. Her mind was screaming at her to do something, anything. She tried the door handle, but it wouldn't budge. Malik must've locked it earlier. She glanced around frantically, searching for some way to escape, but there was nothing but darkness and trees surrounding them.

Her breath came in shallow gasps as her eyes darted over every inch of the car, looking for anything she could use. The glove compartment. The center console. Anything. But it was hopeless. Malik had taken every precaution. Her pulse thundered in her ears as she shifted in her seat, willing her mind to focus. "*Think*," she told herself. "*There has to be a way out.*" Then, her gaze landed on the side mirror, where she spotted the faint reflection of a car with distant headlights coming from the road behind them. Maybe someone was close enough to see. Maybe.

Chapter 8

Niyah's heart raced as she made a quick decision to reach for her phone again, desperately trying to be discreet. She thought if she could just send a quick message, someone would know where she was. But the moment she shifted her hand, Malik's eyes darted to her movements. "What do you think you're doing?" he snapped, his voice laced with suspicion.

She froze, her fingers still hovering over the phone. Her mind raced, scrambling for a believable excuse, but all that came out was a strained laugh. "I—uh, just checking the time," she said quickly, her voice far too steady for the panic swirling inside her. Malik didn't buy it. His eyes narrowed. "You think I'm an idiot?" he growled. "Give me the phone.

Niyah's breath caught in her throat as the words hung in the air. Her mind raced, panic clawing at the edges of her thoughts. She knew she couldn't hand over the phone, not with it still tracking her location. Definitely not with the fragile thread of her escape plan hanging by a single, fraying strand. She could feel the heat of Malik's gaze, the weight of his demand anchoring her in place. He wasn't asking. He was *ordering*.

Her fingers tightened around the phone, almost reflexively, as her mind scrambled for a way out. "No," she said, her voice firmer than she felt. She could hear the trembling edge underneath her words, but she forced herself to hold his stare. "It's just my messages. Nothing important." Her heart raced, and the lie tasted bitter in her mouth, but she had no choice. *Please let him believe me,* she thought desperately.

In an instant, Malik's hand shot forward, grabbing the phone out of her grip. Panic flashed in her eyes as she tried to plead, "Malik, please, don't." But before she could finish, he rolled down the window and hurled her phone into the darkness outside. The phone clattered against the gravel path and disappeared into the brush, swallowed by the night. Her last lifeline was gone.

Niyah's breath caught in her throat, and she felt the walls closing in. She was truly cut off, trapped in the car with someone she no longer recognized. Her eyes darted to him, who was staring at her with a cold, unblinking gaze. Malik's chest rose and fell with deep, deliberate breaths, as if he was trying to rein in his anger.

"You just don't listen, do you?" he muttered, shaking his head. "You think I'm some kind of joke?"

She tried to steady her voice. "No, Malik, I ..."

"Shut up," he interrupted, his tone seething. "You think you can just ignore me and act like I don't matter?"

Fear washed over her, but she tried to keep her voice steady. "I'm not ignoring you. I just... I didn't know what to do."

Malik's jaw tightened, and for a moment, Niyah thought he might snap. "You don't get to make decisions anymore ," he said, his voice low and dangerously calm. "You're going to listen to me now, and only me." Her stomach churned as she realized just how much control he had over her in that moment. It was far more than she was willing to accept.

He let out a bitter laugh and put the car back into gear, going slowly down the narrow path. "You're gonna learn to stop playing games with me," he muttered. "One way or another."

She knew she was running out of time. Niyah had to think fast if she was going to make it out of this situation. She took a deep breath, steeling herself for whatever was to come. "Let me out please," she pleaded. "I promise that I won't call the police either. I just want to get home to my family."

Malik spoke, his tone calm but unyielding. "Stop with all that yelling. It's not going to do you any good. All you need to do is just relax and let me take charge."

Niyah's chest tightened, her breaths coming in short, panicked bursts as she struggled to keep her composure. "I'm not yelling," she whispered in a trembling tone. "I'm just asking for some mercy. Please, I'll do whatever you want, just... just let me go home."

His gaze softened for a brief moment, but it was quickly replaced by the hard edge of control. "You think this is about mercy?" he scoffed, his voice low and menacing. "This is about respect. You'll do what I say, when I say it. Nothing more, nothing less." He reached over, flicking the car's interior light on, and the sharp glow illuminated his face. It was cold and detached, like he was in complete control of the situation. "Now, for the final time, sit back and be quiet. We're not leaving until I'm ready."

She shook her head, now feeling both angry and scared. "Like hell I will. No means no. Now let me out!" She started punching the dashboard, then the windshield and finally her window. She tried her best to find a way to get out, but she was trapped inside. Outside, the park around them silent and foreboding. They were in a spot that she could tell no one could hear her if she cried out for help. She tried to gather her thoughts as she awaited whatever was to come next. Once she heard the doors unlock, she knew it was her chance to get away. But as soon as she had her right foot on the pedal, he grabbed the back of her shirt by the neck and yanked her back.

"Where do you think you're going? As soon as I get what's mine, you're free to go," he said snarling. " I'll even drop you off anywhere you want." She looked at him and raised her right hand to slap him.

"You don't own me or my body. No means no and you will let me go now. Or I promise you that you will regret it," she said angrily.

"Oh, so you're threatening me now, is that it?" he said shoving her against her seat.

Before she could react, he was on top of her ripping her shirt open. He pinned her left wrist on top of the headrest as he tried to unbutton her pants. She felt hopeless for a moment an then she realized that the door was still open. She reached into her purse and pulled out her trusty protector: a small pink, sleek pepper spray canister. "Not a threat, but a promise."

The words barely registered before her hand was already raising the pepper spray, her thumb finding the trigger with frantic precision. Malik's eyes widened in confusion, just a fraction of a second too late. She didn't hesitate as she pressed the nozzle and a burst of stinging mist shot directly into his face. He recoiled, gasping as the burning liquid hit his eyes, the pain instant and overwhelming. His grip loosened on her wrist as his hands flying to his face in a frantic attempt to clear the blinding spray. "Dammit! What the fuck!!"

Niyah didn't waste a moment. With her other hand, she shoved him hard, using every ounce of her remaining strength to push him off of her. As he staggered backward, cursing and stumbling, she jumped out and started running in the direction that they came in. Her goal was to put as much distance between herself and Malik as possible.

She pushed herself forward, her legs burning, her chest tight with fear. She was shaking, but she wasn't about to let herself break down. Not now. Not yet. Every step she took carried her further away from him and closer to freedom. The sound of his shouts still echoed in her ears, but the farther she ran, the quieter they became.

She tripped slightly on an uneven patch of pavement, but she quickly regained her footing and continued moving. The night air was cool, but panic made her skin hot. She sprinted towards the entrance, desperately searching for a way out. The only sounds around her were her pounding heart and Malik's heavy footsteps growing louder behind her.

Chapter 9

"Where do you think you're going?" Malik's voice rang out, furious and breathless. Her pulse quickened even more. She glanced over her shoulder, seeing Malik closing in. His face was a mask of rage, and he was moving faster than she expected.

She tried to run faster, but her strength was declining. Her only hope was the sight of the park entrance, which was a hundred yards away. So close yet out of her reach. Her eyes searched for any weapons like a tree branch that could help her escape from this madman.

Niyah's breath hitched as her legs burned with every desperate stride, the sound of Malik's footsteps growing louder, closer. "*No, not now,*" she thought, her body screaming for relief, but she couldn't slow down. Especially not when the park entrance was so close. The shadows of the trees felt like they were closing in around her. She scanned the ground for anything to use or throw, but the only thing within arm's reach was a thick, jagged rock by the base of a tree.

With no time to think, she grabbed it, her fingers slipping around the rough surface. Malik's footsteps were right behind her now, almost on top of her, but Niyah knew she couldn't let him catch her. Not without a fight. With her breath ragged, she turned and was ready to throw the rock in whatever direction would give her a moment of space. "Stay back!" she shouted, as she raised it above her head.

Malik halted, eyes flashing with a mixture of rage and surprise at the sight of the rock in her hand. He seemed to be calculating, sizing her up, as though deciding whether to charge or back off. Then, with a mocking chuckle, he took a step forward, his expression shifting into something darker. "You really think you can stop me with that?" he sneered, his voice dripping with contempt. "Put it down. It's over."

But she didn't move. Her heart hammered in her chest, the adrenaline surging through her as her grip tightened on the rock. "Stay away from me," she managed, her voice raw but defiant. Her eyes flickered to the park entrance again. It was so close, and yet, with Malik closing in, it felt like a distant, unreachable dream. She had one chance. One shot to get away.

With the entrance ten yards away, she started feeling hopeful. But the closer she was to this, the closer Malik was behind her. He reached out and grabbed the back of her shirt collar. The sudden pull yanked her backwards and she fell on the ground. "You're not going anywhere".

Niyah's body collided with the cold, unforgiving earth, the impact knocking the breath out of her. She gasped, her vision blurring for a split second as she struggled to push herself up. The pain in her hands and knees was sharp, but it was nothing compared to the raw fear coursing through her veins. Malik was already looming over her, his grip tight on the back of her shirt, pulling her closer like a predator reeling in prey.

"Get off me!" she screamed, her hands scrambling for leverage, her legs kicking in the dirt. But Malik's strength was overpowering, and he was unrelenting. His face was inches from hers. "You're not going anywhere," he repeated, his voice low and menacing. He made it sound like a promise of something far worse if she didn't obey.

Niyah scrambled to her feet, her eyes wide with terror. She tried to back away, but he pushes her down again. No sooner than she hit the ground, he was on top of her. "Let's finish what we started earlier in the car." He then pinned both her wrists with his left wrist above her head.

While he was unzipping her pants, she started kicking him. Malik picked up the same rock she dropped. He threatened, "If you continue to fight me, then you will regret it." Niyah, determined to break free, still continued to fight back. The more she struggled, the more he got angrier. He swung the rock down with a brutal force aimed at her head. "Stop fighting me or there's more where this came from." The impact was so hard that she had blood on the side of her face.

She said through clenched teeth, "I'm not going to make it easy for you. I will fight you to my last breath." Hearing those words flared up Malik's rage. He took the rock and started hitting her again. This time with a lot of brute force.

She was still fighting him every bit of the way. Niyah was determined to leave that area. She thought of her kids who gave her strength. In a final attempt, she said weakly "Please .... don't do this. I have a family."

Malik paused for a fraction of a second, as if the mention of her family made him think. For a brief moment, Niyah thought she might have reached him until his lips curled into a twisted smirk. "Family?" he repeated, almost laughing. "Your family's not here. It's just you and me."

The fear that had once been a flicker in her chest now burned like wildfire. Her mind screamed for her to keep fighting, to not let this be the end. She could still hear the faint sound of cars on the main road, distant but real. She wasn't alone. Not yet. She gathered every ounce of strength she had left, meeting his eyes with a desperate fire. "I'll fight you, Malik. I'll never stop fighting."

Malik, thinking about his version of the date, how she flirted and then had him pay for dinner to only go home, flew into a final rage. He put the rock down and started punching her. The force of the punches was enough to knock her unconscious. He felt her stop moving and thought she was using another tactic to trick him. But her eyes were close and she wasn't fighting back anymore. He leaned in to see if she was still breathing and she wasn't.

A chill ran through Malik as he hovered over her, his breath coming in sharp, uneven gasps. The anger still burned through him, but as he looked down at her still form, a creeping panic began to coil in his gut. He had meant to teach her a lesson, to make her understand that no one walks away from him, that no one uses him. The way she had flirted, played him for dinner, and then disappeared. He couldn't stand it. It was supposed to be punishment. *Not this.*

He leaned down and pressed his cheek near Niyah's nose and mouth. Every second felt like an eternity as Malik held his breath hoping for some sign of life. *"Give me a sign that you're still alive"* he pleaded with himself. *"A breath, a twitch, anything."* He tried to find a pulse, but there was nothing. He couldn't believe it. *No. No, this can't be real.* He shook her gently at first, then more urgently, his voice cracking as he called her name. "Niyah, wake up. Wake up!" But the weight of her stillness crushed him in a way he hadn't anticipated. The reality of what he had done started to settle in, but it was too late. There was no going back now.

His mind raced, desperately trying to find a way out of the mess he had created. He thought of the lies or stories he could spin. Or how he could cover it all up and make it seem like an accident, but nothing made sense. His thoughts were chaotic, spiraling in every direction. He knew he had gone too far this time. And no matter what story he told, the truth would haunt him forever.

Malik took out the hand towel he'd used in the car to wipe his eyes and starting wiping his hands and the rock he used. Once he was sure it was clean of his fingerprints and blood, he threw it as far he could. He stood up and started brushing off the grass from his clothes. He couldn't believe what just happened and now his mind was racing with how to fix it without it coming back to him.

Malik glanced over his shoulder to make sure no one else was around before typing out a hurried text to Tony:

"I need you to get here now. Things got out of control."

He hit send, feeling a knot of dread form in his stomach. Malik knew he was in deep, and now he was pulling Tony into it too. But he didn't see another way out. He couldn't just leave her here. He couldn't leave any loose ends.

His phone buzzed almost immediately with Tony's response:

"What do you mean out of control? Where r u?"

Malik's fingers hovered over the screen as he tried to figure out how to explain it. He couldn't bring himself to type everything out. Not in a text.

"Just come to the back entrance of Hidden Oaks. I'll explain when you get here. It's bad, man."

There was no response for a minute. Malik could imagine Tony on the other end, probably cursing under his breath and wondering what kind of mess he had gotten them into. Then, the screen lit up with Tony's reply:

"On my way. This better not be some BS."

Malik let out a shaky breath and pocketed his phone. He tried to collect himself by taking deep breaths to steady his nerves. But there was no turning back now. All he could do was wait and hope that Tony showed up before everything fell apart completely.

Chapter 10

M alik paced back and forth, his nerves wound tighter with each passing second. He couldn't keep still, glancing at his phone every few moments, waiting for a reply from Tony. The night air felt cooler than it was, making him shiver. Not just from the chill, but from the fear that was starting to gnaw at him. Every distant sound, a car passing, a branch snapping, set him on edge making him jump and whip his head around.

"Come on, come on," he muttered under his breath, wiping sweat from his palms. His mind was racing, trying to think of what to do if Tony didn't show up. He had always been able to rely on Tony in tight spots before, but this... this was different. He felt the weight of the situation pressing down on him, the consequences of what he'd done sinking in fully. Malik's breath quickened, his frantic thoughts running wild about what would happen if Tony bailed, or worse, if the police showed up first.

His phone finally buzzed, and he fumbled with it, his fingers shaking. It was a message from Tony:

"Almost there. Sit tight."

Malik took a deep breath, trying to calm himself, but it was no use. He felt like the walls were closing in, and every second felt like an hour. The reality of what he'd done hit him like a punch to the gut, and the panic in his eyes grew as he waited in the darkness for Tony to arrive.

Malik's chest heaved with shallow breaths, the weight of his actions crashing down on him with each passing second. His hands trembled at his sides, his knuckles still raw from the force of the punches. The silence around him felt suffocating, oppressive, and he couldn't shake the image of Niyah's motionless body. It was a nightmare that he couldn't wake up from. *"What the hell have I done?"* The thought circled in his mind like a broken record; but no matter how many times he tried to push it away, it always returned, louder, more insistent.

He glanced at his phone again, hoping for a text from Tony saying he was close, but the screen remained empty. Malik couldn't afford to panic, not yet. He needed to hold it together. He had to keep his composure long enough to clean up the mess he'd made. The plan had always been simple: put her in her place, scare her a little, make her regret thinking she could walk away from him. But now, looking down at the cold, lifeless expression on her face, nothing about it seemed simple anymore.

Tony would know what to do. He always did. Malik tried to convince himself of that, but the dread in his gut kept gnawing at him. He could feel the heaviness of the darkness pressing down, as though it was closing in around him, and the longer he waited, the more it felt like there was no way out. He thought of the lies he would have to tell, the story he would have to craft to cover this up. But deep down, a small voice whispered that no matter how hard he tried, he wouldn't escape what had happened tonight.

The distant glow of headlights pierced through the dark, and Malik's stomach churned. It The distant glow of headlights pierced through the dark, and Malik's stomach churned. It was Tony's car. But instead of relief, all he felt was a growing knot of anxiety. Every second of waiting had only magnified the enormity of what he'd done, and now that Tony was about to arrive, Malik couldn't escape the gnawing realization that there was no easy way out.

As the car rolled closer, Malik wiped his palms on his pants, his breathing quick and shallow. His mind raced, frantically trying to pull together some semblance of a plan. *What was he supposed to say to Tony? What would they do? Would they fix it? Or was it already too late for that?* The headlights came closer, casting long shadows that seemed to stretch and twist in the corners of his vision. The reality was sinking in harder now, faster than he could think. There was no going back.

When the car finally stopped, the engine cut off, and the sound of the doors opening felt like the finality of a sentence. Tony's figure appeared in the dim light, silhouetted by the car's glow, and Malik felt his pulse spike, a cold sweat creeping down his neck. "*What the hell am I supposed to say?*" He wanted to shout, to demand answers from himself, but his voice was caught in his throat. The weight of the decision, the weight of Niyah's life—or death—was pressing down on him, and Tony's arrival only made it feel more real.

Tony stepped out of his car, looking around with a mix of curiosity and concern. "Malik, you okay?" he called out as he approached, his voice carrying a hint of casual friendliness that didn't quite mask his underlying concern.

Malik's heart pounded as he approached Tony, his eyes darting nervously towards the darkened edges of the park. "Tony, thanks for coming," Malik said, his voice strained. "I... I really need your help."

Tony frowned, noting the urgency and fear in Malik's demeanor. "What's going on? You look like you've seen a ghost."

Malik hesitated, glancing around to make sure they were alone. "It's... it's about Niyah," he began, his voice barely above a whisper. "I need you to help me with something... serious."

Tony's expression shifted to one of concern, his eyes narrowing. "Serious? Malik, what happened?"

Malik took a deep breath, his hands trembling. "I didn't mean for this to happen. We had an argument earlier tonight, and it... it got out of hand. I didn't know what I was doing. I—" He stopped, unable to continue, his face pale.

Tony's concern turned to alarm. "Malik, what are you talking about? What happened with Niyah?"

Malik's voice broke as he finally admitted, "I—Niyah's dead. I... I didn't mean to kill her. It was an accident. But now I need help hiding her body. I don't know what to do."

Tony's eyes widened in shock, and he took a step back, his face a mixture of disbelief and anger. "What the hell, Malik? How did this happen?"

Malik looked down at the ground, tears welling up in his eyes. "It was a fight. She was upset, and I just ..." He shook his head, unable to find the words. " I didn't think it would go this far."

Tony ran a hand through his hair, clearly struggling to process the gravity of the situation. "You can't just leave her here, Malik. This is serious. We need to think this through. Do you have any idea what you're asking me to do?"

Malik nodded frantically, his voice pleading. "I know it's messed up, but I'm scared. I don't know how to fix this, and I don't want to go to prison. Please, Tony, I need your help."

Tony's gaze was intense as he tried to assess the situation. "Alright, calm down. We need to figure out a plan, but we have to be careful. First, we need to make sure no one's around. If you've got her somewhere here, we need to get to her before anyone sees us."

Malik nodded, leading Tony to a secluded area of the park, away from the main path. The night was eerily quiet, the only sounds being was their footsteps on gravel and the occasional distant call of a bird. They arrived at a small clearing where her body lay in the open, dried blood around her head.

Tony's face changed suddenly when he saw the body, the reality of the situation sinking in. "Malik, we need to act fast," he said as he gave him a couple of trash bags. "We'll need to get a lot of leaves or debris to cover her. We also need to make sure there's no trace left here." Malik's eyes were filled with desperation as he nodded, taking the bags to collect leaves and debris. The weight of the night's events pressed heavily on him as he walked alongside Tony.

The night was still and unnervingly quiet as Malik and Tony trudged through the park. Once the bags were full, they made their way back to the lifeless body. Tony spoke in a grim and focused voice, "Alright, we need to cover her up as best as we can. The more natural the cover, the better." They began by spreading out the bags of leaves and branches they had collected. The crunch of leaves and the rustling of branches filled the air, mingling with the distant sounds of the city.

Malik knelt beside the body, his hands trembling as he began to carefully place debris over her. He tried to move with a deliberate calm, though every motion felt laden with guilt and dread. Tony worked beside him, his movements methodical and efficient as he arranged the debris to create a natural-looking cover.

As the layers of debris thickened, the body began to disappear beneath the natural camouflage. The mound of leaves and branches gradually took on a more convincing appearance, blending with the surrounding environment. The scene was almost serene, as if nature had simply taken its course.

Tony wiped sweat from his brow, his face tired but resolute. "Alright, I think this should hold up for now. We'll need to be vigilant and make sure no one comes across this area."

Malik, his face still drawn with distress, nodded. "Thank you, Tony. I don't know how to repay you for this."

Tony placed a reassuring hand on Malik's shoulder. "We'll get through this. For now, we need to stay smart and stay quiet. Let's get out of here." They turned and walked to their cars, neither one saying a word.

Chapter 11

Malik drove home in silence, his mind racing with the weight of the night and what lay ahead. The highway stretched out before him, the yellow lines blurring as he pressed down on the gas pedal. The radio was off because he couldn't handle the noise. The only sounds were the steady hum of the engine and his own ragged breathing.

His thoughts were scattered, ping-ponging between flashes of what had happened and the uncertainty of his future. Every red light felt like an eternity, every car that passed seemed to stare, as if they knew. Malik tried to shake off the growing sense of dread gnawing at his insides. He glanced at the rear view mirror occasionally, half-expecting to see flashing lights or the shadowy form of someone following him. It was evident that he was getting paranoid and the paranoia was relentless.

As he drove, Malik's mind replayed the events of the evening in his mind. He wished he could go back and undo everything, but he couldn't and now guilt was starting to weigh heavily on his chest. How had he allowed himself to become someone capable of such a tragedy? He thought of Niyah and her demise. He remembered the moment of impact, the crushing realization that something had gone terribly wrong. It was a reality he could scarcely comprehend, let alone accept. He was overwhelmed with a sense of remorse and self-loathing.

Malik glanced at the passenger seat where the crumpled trash bags lay hidden, remnants of the night's desperate attempt to cover his tracks. The sight of them made his stomach churn. He had covered the body with Tony's help, to make it look like nothing more than a natural part of the park. But in the pit of his stomach, he knew it wasn't enough.

The fear of discovery was a constant gnawing presence. Malik imagined scenarios where the police would come knocking at his door, where the evidence would surface, and where he would have to confront the full weight of his actions. He saw headlines in his mind, stories of the tragic accident, and the inevitable blame that would fall on him. The thought of facing the legal system, of being judged for his actions, was almost unbearable.

He shifted his gaze to the empty road ahead, trying to focus on something, anything, that would distract him from his spiraling thoughts. The streetlights flickered past, casting fleeting shadows across the truck's interior. The steady hum of the engine was the only sound in the truck, almost comforting in its consistency, until his mind raced again, pulling him back into the storm of his thoughts.

Every street he passed seemed to mock him, the normalcy of the city life juxtaposed against the darkness of what he had done. People were going to wake up in a few hours to go through their daily routines, unaware of the tragedy that had unfolded just a short distance away. The contrast felt unbearable. Malik wondered how long it would be before someone discovered what he had done, and what the repercussions would be.

He thought about Tony and whether he should have trusted him at all. He replayed the last moments with her in his mind, her fearful eyes burning into his memory like a brand. "Why did it go so wrong?" he muttered under his breath, his voice cracking slightly. He had never imagined his life would spiral this far out of control.

His thoughts became more chaotic. He imagined scenarios of discovery and arrest, the legal consequences, the faces of those who would be affected by this tragedy. The fear of the unknown future gnawed at him. *What if someone saw them leaving the park? What if evidence was found?*

As he continued to drive, Malik's thoughts turned to Niyah's family. She'd talked about them all the time. The thought of what they would feel if they knew the truth was unbearable. He imagined the grief, the confusion, and the anger that would follow. The burden of their sorrow weighed heavily on him, adding to his already overwhelming sense of guilt.

The truck rolled through a quiet part of town, the streets deserted and silent. Malik's eyes were drawn to the empty spaces, the absence of life that seemed to reflect his own emotional void. The night had become a dark, oppressive canvas on which his fears and regrets were painted in vivid, painful strokes. Each passing streetlight illuminated his face, casting fleeting shadows that mirrored the conflict within him. He didn't know where he was heading, physically or mentally, and it gnawed at him, a constant reminder that he had no control over either. The weight of everything he had said and done tonight pressed down on his chest, making the silence in the truck feel like a suffocating force.

He drove through familiar streets passing landmarks from his past including a playground where he used to play basketball with friends and a corner store where he and his cousin would hang around on hot summer days. Everything seemed both distant and too close, as if his memories and reality were colliding in a strange, surreal way.

Malik finally reached his neighborhood, pulling into the parking lot of his apartment building. He leaned back in his seat and tried to steady his racing thoughts. He took a moment to close his eyes, trying to gather his thoughts, but the weight of everything felt like a thousand stones pressing down on him. And for the first time in his life, he wasn't sure if he was strong enough to carry it. When he finally stepped out of the car, he felt like he was moving in slow motion. He walked up to the front door, hesitating for a second before pushing it open.

The familiarity of his dimly lit living room and the comfort of his apartment seemed like a fragile illusion. He glanced around, half-expecting the walls to close in on him. He sank into his favorite chair and turned on the TV for background noise. As the room grew colder and the shadows lengthened, Malik realized that no matter how carefully they had staged the crime scene, the true crime was the loss of his peace of mind.

Chapter 12

Janelle laid in bed staring at the ceiling, her mind racing. She couldn't shake the worry about her sister not checking in. She didn't want to wake her husband Darren, who was peacefully asleep beside her, but the anxiety continued to grow. She tossed and turned, her mind racing despite her exhaustion.

She rolled over to pick up her phone from the bedside table. Her heart sank as she looked at an empty screen. This only deepened her unease. She thought about all the times they had stayed up late talking and laughing, and how it felt different this time.

She knew her sister was not a morning person, but she still needed to hear her voice. She decided to call her but strangely, it went straight to voicemail. "It's me. Call me when you wake up." She didn't remember hearing it ring a few times. She called back again to make sure. "*It never goes straight to voicemail,*" she thought. "*This is strange. She never turns her phone off. It's always on.*"

The nagging feeling was getting to her again. She had to do something, so she got up out of bed and went to the kitchen. Janelle couldn't concentrate on anything else but her sister so she made a pot of coffee to keep her mind busy. When she was finished, she grabbed her favorite mug and sat in the recliner in the living room. She tried Niyah's number again, and like before, it went to voicemail.

Janelle was lost in thought when she heard a car door slam outside. It barely registered in her mind, as her street was always busy on weekends. Cars and neighbors coming and going weren't unusual in the slightest. She stared out the window, her mind going over the events from the day before, trying to make sense of things. The uneasy feeling lingered, and she couldn't shake it.

Suddenly, the doorbell rang sharply, echoing through the quiet house. Janelle jumped, the sound jolting her out of her reverie. She frowned, wondering who could be visiting so early in the morning. She opened the door and saw her niece Myia standing there.

"What's wrong sweetie," she asked looking at her niece's tired face. "You've been crying. Is everything okay?" Myia hesitated before answering. "My mom didn't come home last night. She was supposed to watch Aiyden so I could go to work, but when I went to her room...it looked like she never came back home."

Janelle felt her heart drop into her stomach. She looked at Myia, eyes wide, trying to make sense of what she was hearing. "Wait ... what do you mean never came home? You mean from last night?"

Myia nodded, biting her lip to keep it from trembling. "I thought that she went out early this morning or ... " she faltered. "But her bed's made and it looks like she never slept in it."

Janelle sat down across from her niece, feeling the weight of the situation settle over her. "I've been worried about her too. I called and texted numerous times and didn't get a response,"she said worriedly.

"I did too auntie, and it keeps going to voicemail," Myia replied, barely above a whisper. "She never leaves it off. Should I call the police?"

"We know that the police isn't going to do anything this early. Give it some time. She could be on the way home. If she hasn't come home by this afternoon, let me know."

Myia stood up. "We need to do something now. I can't wait until later. It could be too late." Her aunt walked over to hug her.

"Calm down sweetie. Take a deep breath. What we can do now is call around. Hopefully if they see her, they will tell her to check in with us." Myia nodded, her expression now determined. "Okay I'll start calling her friends."

While Myia was calling around, Janelle went to her phone searching for a recent photo. She was going to make a post on social media. When she found the one that she wanted to use she began typing:

'Hey everyone, I need your help. My sister hasn't come home since last night and we're really worried about her. If you see her, tell her to call home or call her sis. We need to know if she's okay.'

She added the photo and tapped the 'Post' button. She also tagged everyone that was at Zara's place yesterday. Now all they could do was wait and pray that someone will see her and she will come home. Almost immediately, her phone starts buzzing with notifications; likes, shares, and comments. Her two oldest called her on a group call. Marcus told her he was already on the way there, while Jordan said he'll check in on his way to work.

It had been hours since Niyah didn't come home, and every moment seemed to drag on with the weight of uncertainty. Janelle, Myia, and the rest of the family had spent the rest of the day combing through the places she might have gone; her favorite spots, the homes of friends, anywhere that seemed plausible. But every stop was met with disappointment, and every call ended with the same empty words: "No, we haven't seen her."

They had even driven through old neighborhoods and past spots that Niyah was known to frequent. The two brothers tried their best to stay positive, throwing out ideas of where she might have gone or whom she might have met. By the evening, the exhaustion from fruitless searching and the dread of not knowing what had happened took a toll.

Janelle's mind raced, every scenario worse than the last. She replayed every conversation, every detail she could remember from the night, but nothing made sense. How had things escalated so quickly? Her older sister had been out on a date with someone they didn't know well, but she never expected it would end like this.

Janelle pulled the car over. "We need to go to the police," she said firmly, her voice cracking slightly. It was a declaration none of them wanted to make, but it was the only step left. Myia placed a gentle hand on her aunt's shoulder, nodding in agreement. "We've done all we can," she whispered. "I'll text the others to meet us there."

With a heavy sigh, Janelle turned the key in the ignition and drove the rest of the way in silence, Myia quietly holding Aiyden in the backseat. She knew that once they walked through the doors of the police station, there was no turning back. It was a step they had been avoiding. Each of them hoping the situation might resolve itself without needing to confront the truth. But now, with the looming reality ahead of them, there was no more room for hesitation. Janelle's grip tightened on the steering wheel as she glanced in the rearview mirror, meeting Myia's eyes for a brief, silent exchange of understanding. No words were needed. Neither of them could afford to break down now, not when they had to be strong for the family.

When they finally arrived at the police station, the world outside seemed to stand still. The building loomed large and impersonal, the fluorescent lights flickering above them as they walked in. The quiet hum of the air conditioning and the murmur of voices from behind the desks did nothing to ease the anxiety that clung to their every step.

Inside, the officer at the front desk looked up as they approached, his expression unreadable. "How can I help you?" he asked in a clipped tone.

"We're here to report a missing person," Janelle said, her voice steady but strained. Myia stood next to her holding Aiyden.

The officer raised an eyebrow, his fingers poised over the keyboard. "Who's missing?"

"Niyah Thompson," Myia answered quickly, her voice calm but with an edge of desperation that barely concealed the fear in her eyes.

The officer nodded and gestured for them to sit. "Take a seat. Someone will be with you shortly."

They sat down in the sterile waiting area, the uncomfortable silence pressing in around them. Myia sat in a stiff plastic chair, her fingers tapping nervously against the armrest. She had her phone out, glancing at it every few seconds as if willing it to ring. She was hoping that there would be a message; something, anything; that would let her know that her mom was okay. Then her mind began to fill with questions. *"What if they couldn't find her mother? What if something had happened to her?"* She glanced over at her aunt and noticed that something was not quite right with her.

Janelle's gaze was fixed on the desk ahead, her eyes distant and unfocused, like she wasn't really here. It was as if she was caught somewhere else entirely, her mind elsewhere. Myia opened her mouth to speak, but then she hesitated. What could she say? They were there because of Niyah, but it felt like there was something more pressing consuming Janelle, something Myia couldn't place.

"Nelly," Myia said softly, her voice tentative. "Are you okay?"

Janelle didn't immediately respond. She just blinked, like she was snapping out of some trance. Then, she turned to Myia, forcing a smile that didn't reach her eyes. "Yeah, I'm fine. Just... worried, you know?"

Myia studied her aunt for a moment, and noticed that there was more going on than just concern for her mom. Myia pressed on, her voice quieter this time.

"You're not fine, Nelly. I can tell something's wrong." She hesitated, feeling the weight of her words. "Is there something you're not telling me?"

Janelle's eyes flicked to the floor, and for a moment, Myia thought she might break down right there. But instead, she took a deep breath, a shaky one, and exhaled slowly, looking back up at Myia with a look that was both apologetic and frustrated. "There's something that I haven't told you guys yet. I've been trying to keep it together, but—"

Just then, the door to the back office opened, and a tall, burly, stern-looking officer appeared. "Ms. Thompson?" he said, addressing Janelle.

Janelle stood up immediately, her legs almost buckling beneath her. "Yes, that's us," she replied, voice cracking

We'll need to take a statement," the officer said, motioning for them to follow him.

Chapter 13

As they walked into the office, Janelle felt the weight of the moment pressing down on her. She had never imagined it would come to this. She had always been the one in control, the one everyone leaned on. But now, as she sat in that small, cold room, she felt completely out of her depth. Myia sat next to her, squeezing her hand as the officer began to introduce himself.

"Before we go any further," he said, his voice steady but gentle, "I should introduce myself properly. My name is Officer Harris, and I'm with the Crest Ridge Police Department's Missing Persons Unit." He extended his hand to her, and Janelle shook it, a bit stiffly, but she appreciated the gesture. "I know this is a difficult time, but I want you to know that you're in good hands. My team and I take cases like this very seriously," he continued, his eyes not leaving hers. "I'll be personally overseeing the search for your sister, and I won't stop until we find her."

Janelle nodded, though a part of her was still skeptical. She wanted to believe him, to trust that the police could help, but she couldn't. Her emotions were too raw and the fear gnawing at her stomach made it hard to hold on to hope. "I just... I don't know what to think," she admitted quietly, voice breaking slightly. "She's always been independent. This isn't like her."

Officer Harris's expression softened with understanding. "I can imagine how terrifying this must be. But I need you both to stay focused. We're going to get through this. So let's start with the basics. How long has she been missing?"

Myia took a deep breath, her voice quavering as she spoke. "My mother hasn't come home since last night and we haven't heard anything."

Janelle added, "She went out with a guy she met online and she never came back. We've tried calling her phone, but it goes straight to voicemail."

"Do you know what was his name?" Officer Harris asked.

Myia shook her head. "She only gave us a first name, Malik. She told me that she would be back home so I could go to work. When I woke up this morning I noticed that she wasn't there. So I went to my aunt's house to see if she heard from her. When she said she didn't, then we knew something was wrong. She's never done that before. We've tried her friends and called all the places she usually goes, but no one has seen her."

"Has she ever gone missing before?" Officer Harris inquired, glancing up.

"No, never," she answered, her voice trembling. "She's always been really good about letting us know if she's running late or if plans change. This isn't like her at all." Officer Harris nodded, jotting down notes. "Okay, we'll need to gather some more information. Does she have any medical conditions or anything that might be relevant?"

Myia shook her head again, the tears she had been holding back threatening to spill over. "She got some tattoos on her arms and legs. I just don't understand where she could be."

The officer gave her a sympathetic look. "If you have a recent picture of her or her tattoos, I'm going to need them. It will help us with the search."

Myia reached into her purse and pulled out a crumpled photo. It was a picture of her mother at a reunion a few weeks ago. Niyah was smiling brightly. "Here," Myia said, handing it over. Officer Harris took the photo and examined it briefly before placing it in a file. "Thank you. We're going to enter this information into our system and start the search process. Given that she's been missing for a full day, we'll escalate the case."

Myia's eyes were locked on the officer's face, desperation clear in her gaze. "What does that mean? Will the police start searching for her now? Will they put out an alert?"

"Yes," Officer Harris assured her. "We'll issue a missing persons alert and contact local authorities. We'll also get in touch with the media to help spread the word. We'll be doing everything we can to find her."

Myia, trying to hold back the tears, "What if... what if she doesn't come back? What if something's happened to her?"

Officer Harris replied in a reassuring voice, "We understand your fear, and it's important to stay hopeful. The sooner we act, the better the chances of finding her safe. You'll need to stay available for any updates and continue to provide us with any new information that might come up."

"I will," Myia promised. "I'll do whatever I can to help."

Janelle responded, " We just want her to come home." They stood up to leave. Officer Harris watched them walk away, his face a mask of professional concern. He knew the chances of finding someone missing for only a few hours were often good, but the look on Myia's face made him more aware of the gravity of her situation. As they walked outside to join the others, Myia took out her phone contemplating on calling her mom one more time. She knew it was pointless since it would go straight to voicemail anyway.

The two women walked out the doors and the family's eyes turned to them immediately.

"Hey," Myia said, her voice trembling slightly. "We're back."

Marcus looking anxious, "What's the news? Did the police say anything?"

Myia took a deep breath, "We've filed the missing persons report. The police have all the information about my mom, and they said that they will start the search."

Zara's eyes filled with tears, "Did they say what happens next? What are they doing to find her?"

Janelle answered, "They're issuing an alert and contacting local authorities. They're also going to work with the media to spread the word. We've been assured that they're taking this very seriously and will do everything they can."

Marcus said, "Well that's not enough. It feels like they don't really care. If it were a white family, would it be different?" Everyone looked at him. He was saying what they all were thinking. "They're not going to put any effort in trying to find her. It's all on us to do it." He took his keys out of his pocket and grabbed his phone. "I'm going back out to search."

"Son, it's dark. We've have been out searching all day. It's not safe."

"That's exactly why I need to go. What if she's out there hurt? I know my aunt. She'd do the same for me."

"You've barely ate today. You need to rest. Your body needs to rejuvenate itself."

"I can't rest and I can't sit around doing nothing. I need to get back out there."

He looked at his mom and saw the tears in her eyes. "Remember she is more than your aunt, she's also my sister. My only sister. I don't know what I would do if she isn't found. But I also need to be strong for my parents as well."

"Well, since he's not going, then I will. She's my rock," Zara said.

"Zara you need to finish getting settled in. We'll call you when we hear something," she said tiredly. "As a matter of fact, let's all go home, get some rest, and meet back up in the morning."

They reluctantly agreed and started walking towards their cars. Once Janelle reached her car, her steps slowed. The overwhelming weight of fear, worry, and exhaustion had finally caught up to her. She wrapped her arms around herself, staring blankly at the pavement beneath her feet. The world seemed to blur, the sounds of cars and faint conversations fading into the background as she struggled to breathe steadily.

Darren walked up beside her, his face etched with concern. "Hey," he said softly, placing a comforting hand on her back. She didn't respond, just continued to wipe at her tears, feeling utterly drained.

He didn't push her to speak, understanding she needed a moment. After a while, he gently said, "Babe, you've been running around for hours. Let me drive you home, alright?" She shook her head slightly, as if trying to protest, but the words wouldn't come. Deep down, she knew he was right; she couldn't do much more by standing in the parking lot, but leaving felt like giving up.

"Let me drive you home," Darren repeated, his voice firmer this time, but still gentle. He turned her towards him and held her shoulders, looking into her eyes. "We're all scared, and we'll stay on top of this. You need to rest too. Let's go home."

Janelle finally nodded, letting out a shaky breath. She felt Darren's arm wrap around her as he led her to the car. She didn't say anything, just leaned on him as they walked, grateful for the support and the small sense of direction amidst the chaos. As they got into the car, Janelle took one last glance at the police station, silently praying for answers before they drove away.

She was so lost in thought leaving the police station that she didn't realize that they were pulling up to their house. She opened her door and got out. She looked at Darren as he opened the driver side door, "Thank you for being here with me. I don't know how I'd get through this without you."

Darren walked around the car to give her a tight hug, "No need to thank me. I'll always be here for my baby. This will pass and you will find out that she has been safe all along." He held her close as she tilted her head back to look at the sky, her lips moving in a silent prayer. She closed her eyes tightly, hoping that some peace or clarity would come. Darren, sensing the depth of her turmoil, didn't say anything. He just held her close, letting her cry and take the time she needed.

Chapter 14

The family gathered at Niyah's the next morning waiting for news from the police. Myia sat at the kitchen table with her son Aiyden. His small fingers clutched the edges of his tablet, his little face illuminated by the bright colors and animated characters dancing on the screen. Despite the cartoon's cheerful soundtrack, his brows were furrowed, a mix of concentration and concern evident on his tiny face. "Mom, look!" he said, his voice high and eager. He tilted the tablet so she could see the cartoon characters.

Myia's gaze flickered briefly to the tablet before drifting back to her phone. Her exhaustion was palpable; dark circles underlined her eyes, and her movements were slow and mechanical. She nodded absently trying to force a smile that didn't quite reach her eyes. "That's nice, Aiyden," she murmured, her voice lacking its usual warmth.

Aiyden's small fingers tapped on the tablet screen as he tried to show her a specific part of the video, hoping to share the joy he found in it. "Look, Mommy! The funny part's coming up!" Myia reached over and placed a hand on Aiyden's small arm, squeezing it lightly. "I'm sorry, baby, but mommy's really tired right now." His little face fell slightly as he turned back to the screen. "My GiGi would love to see this. When is she coming home?" The mention of her mom brought a fresh wave of sadness over her. Myia, trying to hold in tears, "Hopefully, soon. She'll be home before you know it."

Janelle leaned against the doorway, not wanting to interrupt. She had been watching the interaction and it reminded her of the importance of family. Myia glanced up and noticed Janelle standing there, a slight look of surprise crossing her face. "Hey, Auntie," she greeted silently.

"Hey," Janelle replied softly, "Have you heard anything yet?"

"We haven't heard anything yet and I'm really getting worried now." Taking her hand, Janelle said tiredly,"I'm sure we'll hear something today. I have faith that we will."

"But auntie, I can't just sit here and do nothing. I want my mom to come home. Should I go back by the police station today? I don't understand what's taking so long. They should have heard something by now."

"I think you should give them a chance, sweetie. As a matter of fact, Marcus and Zara will start searching this morning. Why don't I take Aiyden to my house and you can go with them."

In the living room, Tyson sat on the edge of the couch, his phone pressed to his ear. His eyes were tired, but his voice remained steady as he made call after call, hoping for any information that could lead them to his mother. Each call ended with the same disheartening answer, nothing. He leaned back and ran a hand over his face, trying to mask the frustration building up inside him.

He had to get out the house before he went stir crazy so he walked in the kitchen. "Nelly, I'll go with you." he said as he walked towards Aiyden. "Hey buddy, let's get your stuff together. We're going to Auntie's house."

"Yay!" he said running to his room. He came bounding back into the kitchen, his small feet padding quickly against the tile floor. Everyone turned their heads, their eyes following him as he skidded to a stop. He hesitated for a second, nervously shifting his weight from one foot to the other.

"Will grandma be here when I get back?" The question hung in the air, freezing everyone in place. Myia's eyes welled up with tears, but she forced a smile for her son. Darren stopped in the middle of reaching for his coffee cup. Janelle, standing in the doorway, felt her heart clench at the question. Tyson walked over to him, bent down and said, "We're all hoping she comes back soon, buddy."

As Aiyden shuffled out of the kitchen to gather his things, the silence in the room remained heavy. Myia let out a shaky breath, wiping the corner of her eye with her sleeve. Darren glanced at Janelle, who was still standing at the doorway, her arms crossed as if trying to shield herself from the reality of the situation. Tyson looked between them, his jaw tense.

"He's picking up on everything," Myia finally said, breaking the silence. "He knows something's wrong, even if he doesn't really understand what."

Janelle nodded slowly, "Kids always do. They're more aware than we give them credit for."

Tyson leaned back against the counter, crossing his arms. "We can't keep pretending like he doesn't know, though. Every time he asks about Mom, we're just avoiding the truth."

Darren rubbed the back of his neck, his eyes trained on the doorway where Aiyden had disappeared. "He's so young. He's gonna ask questions, and I don't know how we're supposed to answer them."

Myia sighed. "I don't even know what to say to him. He keeps asking if Mom is coming back and...it's like each time, I feel this lump in my throat because I can't tell him what he wants to hear."

Janelle uncrossed her arms and walked over to the table, sitting down heavily. "We just have to be there for him," she said, her voice barely above a whisper. "Even if we don't have answers...we just have to let him know he's not alone."

Tyson nodded, his expression softening. "He's scared," he said, his voice filled with a mixture of sadness and frustration. "And honestly, so are we."

For a moment, they all sat in that shared silence, feeling the weight of the situation, the uncertainty, and the fear of what might come next. The sound of Aiyden running back, ready to go, eased the tension.

That evening, Janelle couldn't shake the gnawing worry in her chest. Aiyden has finally drifted off to sleep on the couch, exhausted from playing games all day. The sight of his peaceful face tugged at her heartstrings . All day she kept busy around the house fussing over chores that didn't need doing. She decided to call and check on Marcus. After a few rings, he answered, his voice steady but tinged with concern.

"Hey, ma. I was just about to call you."

"Have you heard anything ?"

"No, nothing yet. I drove all around town and didn't see her. I even asked, but no one's seen her. We're still waiting on updates."

"We're getting really worried. Aiyden is even asking when is she coming home."

"I heard. Myia's been riding with Zara and me all day. I know that it has to be so hard on her. We're doing everything we can to find her, I promise."

After a few more minutes of conversation, she hung up. She looked at Aiyden and gently adjusted the blanket around him. She sat down beside him and grabbed her laptop. Janelle wanted to search for any new updates or leads, but there was none. She said to herself, "It's almost been two days and no one has heard anything. Not even the police. Where could she be?"

Memories of her sister flooded her mind; her sister's laughter, her warmth, and the way she always knew how to make things better. *"I can't let her down. "* she swallowed hard. She vowed to herself that she will continue to search and will keep fighting until they find her sister. Her heart ached as she contemplated the weight of that promise.

She knew she couldn't shield them from every storm, but she can be the lighthouse guiding them through. She wiped a stray tear from her cheek, a quiet resolve settling in. "We will find you."

Chapter 15

Myia walked into the house, pushing the door open quietly, half-expecting to find her mom awake and waiting for her in the living room. The house was dark, with only the soft glow of the kitchen light spilling into the hallway. She paused for a moment, listening for any sounds of movement, but the house was eerily still.

"Mom?" she called out, her voice echoing slightly in the silence. She kicked off her shoes. The house remained silent. She had hoped to see her mom coming out of her room or on the back porch smoking. "Where are you?" Myia whispered to herself. She thought back to the last time they were together. She wished she could go back in time and tell her she loves her. She went back to the living room, where Marcus was sitting on the couch.

"I thought you were going home," she said as she plopped down.

"You think that I would leave my favorite cousin alone tonight?"

They settled into a comfortable silence, munching on chips as the TV played in the background. Myia glanced at Marcus, who seemed lost in thought, his gaze distant as he stared at the screen without really watching it. She felt a flicker of gratitude for having him by her side. They'd been through so much together, shared moments of joy, of pain, of uncertainty. In a way, it was comforting to know that no matter where life took them, they had each other to fall back on. She looked at him again, silently appreciating the quiet solidarity between them, before turning her attention back to the TV, letting the peacefulness of the moment wash over her.

"Remember when we used to sneak snacks and watch movies in your room?" he asked. She chuckled, "How could I forget? Mom always caught us! But she'd just laugh and let us stay up late."

"And she ended up telling us wild stories about her childhood," Marcus added, "I miss that." They reminisced about those nights growing up. As the cousins continued their lighthearted banter, the atmosphere in the living room feels warmer and more relaxed. Just as Myia leaned back into the couch, her phone buzzed on the coffee table, breaking the moment. She glanced down and read a message from Tyson:

"On my way there. Got something to lighten the mood!"

A grin spreads across her face as she types back quickly,

"Perfect timing! Come on over!"

She looks up at Marcus, who raises an eyebrow, curious about the text. "Looks like Tyson's on the way," Myia said, her excitement bubbling over. Marcus nodded, a playful glint in his eyes. "Awesome! The more, the merrier. I have a little surprise too." He reached into his pocket, the mischievous smile returning as he pulled out a sizable bag of cigarillos and a big pouch of weed. "Thought we could roll a blunt while we wait for Tyson. It's supposed to be great for stress relief."

"Let's do it," she agrees, feeling the weight of the day begin to lift. As Marcus prepared to roll the blunt, she looked at her phone hoping that Tyson would arrive soon. He finished rolling the blunt just as Tyson walked in the door. He was holding a small bag of weed. "Great minds think alike," he said looking at the table.

He held up the freshly rolled blunt and held it up triumphantly. "Voila! The perfect blunt!" Tyson's eyes light up with enthusiasm. "Absolutely!" he said sitting on the edge of the coffee table. Marcus lit the blunt and took a big drag, letting the smoke fill his lungs then exhaling a cloud that dissipated into the air. "Who's next?" Myia took it out of his hand, took a drag and then passed it to Tyson.

They continued passing the blunt to each other, the faint smell of the herb filling the air. "I can't believe how much I missed doing this with y'all," Myia said, a relaxed smile spreading across her face. "It's been awhile" he agreed. "We've got to make it a regular thing. This is what cousins are for."

"Do you know what else cousins are for?" Tyson started. "They're for ordering food. I'm hungry." Myia laughed as she replied, "I'm down for that, too. Who's paying?" They both looked at Marcus as he laid back on the couch staring at the ceiling. "Cough cough."

"Oh something must be caught in your throat." He chuckled as he picked up his phone. "Where are we ordering from? Pizza, seafood, Chinese?" They couldn't decide on a place so they ended up with pizza since it would have been delivered the quickest.

While they waited for the food, they were brought briefly back to their situation. "Do you think my mom will be found," Tyson asked softly as the smoke surrounded them. "She'll be fine. And then she's gonna scream about why this room is full of smoke. " Myia answered. They laughed again and continued to share memories, reminiscing about past summers spent laughing, playing, and the silly pranks they pulled on each other.

When they finished the pizzas, Tyson rolled up his blunt and the cycle started again. As the night wore on, Myia found solace. The laughter, the shared stories, and the simple act of being together created a space where they could breathe. Eventually, as they finished the blunt and the laughter faded into a comfortable silence. Myia leaned back on the couch and looked at the other two. She felt a sense of gratitude. They were here for each other and she felt calm it made her feel good. "Pizza and weed are the best combination for family crisis management."

"Agreed. now let's make a pact," Marcus said. "No matter what happens, we'll always find time for moments like this. To take care of each other." Myia and Tyson said at the same time, "Deal." They settled back into their spots, the mood lightening as they passed the joint around.

The hours stretched on, the room filled with laughter, smoke, and the warmth of good company. Myia felt the heaviness of the day begin to fade, replaced by the comforting presence of her brother and cousin. It was strange how a night that had started with uncertainty and fear could shift into something so much lighter. The comfort of shared memories, the familiarity of their jokes and banter, made her forget—if only for a few hours—the gnawing anxiety that had kept her on edge since her mom went missing.

The pizza boxes sat empty, the last slices devoured, and Tyson's blunt had made its rounds once more. It wasn't until the smoke cleared and the food coma started setting in that Myia allowed herself to sink deeper into the couch, her limbs heavy with the combination of relaxation and exhaustion. She glanced at the both of them, who were both visibly more relaxed now. Marcus was leaning back, eyes half-lidded, his fingers tapping to some silent rhythm. Tyson was scrolling through his phone, his usual energy dialed down a few notches, as though the comfort of the moment had settled into his bones as well.

"You know," Tyson began, his voice quieter than usual, "it's crazy to think we all just kinda came together like this. I mean, it feels like no time has passed, but a lot of time has, huh?"

Marcus chuckled softly. "Yeah. It's like we just pick up where we left off. No matter what's happening in our lives, we always come back to this." He looked over at Myia, his expression softening. "I'm glad you called me tonight. You didn't have to do that. You could've just been with my mom, or I don't know, gone through this alone."

Myia smiled faintly, feeling a warmth flood her chest. "I needed this. We all do." She met both their eyes, her heart swelling with appreciation for the bond they shared. "I'm lucky to have you both."

The words hung in the air for a moment, and the trio fell into a comfortable silence again, the only sound being the faint hum of the ceiling fan above them.

Chapter 16

The next morning, Myia woke up on her couch with a throbbing headache, the effects of smoking with Marcus and Tyson still lingering. She rubbed her temples, trying to shake off the discomfort. Last night had been a haze of anxiety, conversations, and smoke-filled air. She knew she needed to focus, but the headache was making it hard to think clearly She glanced at her phone, hoping for a missed call or message from her mom but there was nothing.

Her phone buzzed violently on the coffee table, jolting her out of her thoughts. She glanced at the screen to see a message from her aunt:

"If you're up and about, I've made breakfast. Come over and eat with us. We also need to talk."

A knot formed in her stomach and she quickly got dressed. Myia walked over to Tyson and nudged him with her foot. "Ty, wake up," she muttered. He stirred, groaning in protest before sitting up, rubbing his eyes. His dreadlocks hung messily in front of his face as he looked around, disoriented.

"What's going on?" he said groggily. "It's too early to be up. My head hurts."

"Nelly just sent me a text that she's making breakfast and she wanted to talk to us."

"Why we gotta head over there? You can make me something here and we don't even have to change clothes."

"Let's just go. I ain't got the energy to do anything else," Myia said, grabbing her keys.

The drive over felt agonizingly slow, each minute stretching into eternity. The streets were eerily quiet, the world around her moving on as if nothing had happened. She couldn't understand how life could continue when her mother was missing. As she pulled up to her aunt's house, she spotted Marcus leaning against the porch railing, "Hey, Myia," he said, his voice low and heavy with worry. "You okay?"

"Not really," she admitted, stepping onto the porch. "Have you heard anything?" He shook his head, "No, nothing yet. Mom called the police again this morning. They're still looking for her."

"Okay, is anyone else coming? I know she said she was making breakfast."

"Yeah, Zara is on her way as we speak. She should have already been here by now," he said as they walked in the front door.

Inside the kitchen, Aiyden was sitting at the table next to Darren excitedly telling him about the new season of the anime that was coming out. The smell of fresh coffee and pancakes and syrup filled the air. Janelle bustled around the kitchen, flipping pancakes and pouring chocolate milk, her movements steady despite the weight of worry etched on her face.

She had decided to cook this morning, hoping that the simple act of preparing a meal would distract her from the gnawing worry that had settled deep within. She glanced at Aiyden, who was giggling at a corny joke that Darren told. The innocence of his laughter brought a bittersweet smile to her lips.

"Morning," Janelle said as they shuffled into the kitchen.

"Everything smells good but I think I need some meat this morning," Myia jokingly said.

"I'm not going to torture everyone today," she answered, turning to face her niece. "I cooked bacon, eggs, and pancakes. It's the least I can do."

Myia took some bacon off the plate and went to the table. "Is Aiyden behaving?"

"He's been a little angel, unlike the bacon thief," she replied, chuckling softly. "But how is my favorite niece today. Don't tell Zara I said that."

"I'm hanging in there, auntie. I just don't know what to do without my mom." Just then, Zara ran in the kitchen with her kids "Sorry I'm late!" she panted. "Ooh it looks good," as she looked at the plates. "Is there anything that I need to do?"

"I'm finishing up now," she said as she plated the food, carefully arranging everything before bringing it to the table. The sight of the breakfast spread, golden pancakes, crispy bacon, fluffy scrambled eggs, and steaming cups of coffee had everyone grabbing the paper plates. Aiyden was already reaching for a pancake and biting into it.

"Dig in, everyone!" Janelle said, feeling a flicker of pride as she sat down with them. She poured herself a cup of coffee, savoring the rich aroma as she took a sip. She thought about the Christmas mornings when the whole family would come over for breakfast, then open up the gifts she bought. Times like these were bittersweet. She loved seeing all of them together, but Niyah wasn't there either. She couldn't really be happy until she hears something.

After breakfast, the adults gathered in the living room and the kids went to the den to play video games. Myia, Marcus and Tyson settled onto the couch. Zara sat on the love seat and Darren was in his recliner.

As Janelle sat down next to Zara, she looked from Myia to Tyson, and finally to Marcus "I don't want y'all worrying too much, okay?

I've been making calls, trying to find out where she is. But we need to be patient. The police—"

"Two days, Nelly," Myia interrupted, her voice strained. "She's been gone two days, and nobody knows anything. What if something happened?"

Her face softened. "I know, baby. I know. But we can't jump to the worst conclusions just yet. Your mom's strong. She's been through worse."

Tyson clenched his jaw. "She's never been gone like this before, though. She always comes home."

Silence hung between them for a moment before Janelle responded softly. "We're gonna find her. But until we do, y'all need to stay strong. We can't fall apart now. You hear me?"

Marcus, who had been quiet, finally spoke up. "You think the cops are even looking for her?"

Her expression hardened slightly. "I made sure they are. But we might have to do some of this ourselves."

Zara looked at her aunt, "What do you mean?"

" We need to go look for her ourselves."

"Exactly," Myia said, "Marcus, Zara, do you think you can cover the areas near your place? Talk to your neighbors, see if anyone has seen anything?"

He nodded, "Yeah, we can take my car. Zara and I will check every corner we can think of."

Myia turned to Tyson, "You can ride with me."

"Yeah, I'm in," Tyson said, his voice steady. "We'll head in the opposite direction. We can cover more ground that way."

"Bet," Myia said. "Don't forget to check in."

"Sounds like y'all got it," Janelle interjected. "I'll stay here and watch the kids. I can help coordinate from this end. I've already called my job and told them it's a family emergency and that I won't be in."

"Thanks, Nelly," Myia said. "We'll keep you updated."

Everyone moved to gather their things. Marcus grabbed his keys from the counter while Zara slipped on her jacket.

"Let's meet back here in three hours," Myia said, her voice firm. "If we find anything, we'll regroup and decide what to do next."

They were finally taking action, but the uncertainty of what they might find loomed heavy in her mind.

"Drive safe, okay?" Janelle called out, her voice tinged with worry.

"We will," Myia replied, giving her aunt a reassuring smile before stepping outside.

As Myia got into her car with Tyson, the weight of the morning's conversation still hung heavy in her chest. Her stomach twisted with a mixture of dread and determination. The air felt different today, thicker even, as if the universe itself was holding its breath along with her. It was hard to believe that just two days ago, her life had felt somewhat normal. It was busy and chaotic even, but normal.

Now, each minute felt like it was stretching into eternity, and the thought that her mother could still be out there took over Myia's every waking moment. Someone out there had to know something. They just needed to find that person. Tyson slid into the passenger seat and adjusted his seat belt. "You good?" he asked, his voice quieter than usual, as he turned toward her.

Myia nodded, though the anxiety swirling in her gut made the motion feel mechanical. "Yeah. Just need to keep moving. I don't know how long I can just sit here and wait anymore." She gripped the steering wheel tighter. "I need to find her."

Tyson didn't say anything at first, but she could feel his presence beside her, steadying her. He leaned back in his seat, eyes on the road ahead. "We'll find her, Myia. We're covering a lot of ground today, and the more people we get looking, the faster we'll have answers. Just... don't lose hope, alright?"

She glanced over at him, offering a small smile, grateful for his words even if they didn't feel like they could fill the hole of uncertainty in her heart. Tyson had a way of staying calm when everything around him felt like it was coming apart, and it helped her to hold onto that thread of steadiness. The drive was quiet as Myia thought about all the places they needed to check. She knew that the more ground they covered, the better. They were determined to leave no stone unturned.

Chapter 17

As they drove through the familiar streets, Myia couldn't help but glance over at Tyson. "What do you think we should focus on first?" she asked. "Let's start at North side." he said. "She's always hanging out there with her friends." She proceeds to head in that direction. They went down every street and side street that they knew she frequented.

They drove to the neighborhood store and pulled into an empty spot. "Why are we here?" Tyson asked. "We're going to go in and ask everyone in the store if they've seen Mom," she said as she opened the car door. She approached a couple at a register "Excuse me," she said, her heart racing. "Have you seen this woman?" She pulled out her phone, showing them a picture of Niyah. They both shook their heads, their expressions sympathetic but unhelpful. "I'm sorry, we haven't seen her," the woman replied softly.

"Thank you," Myia said, forcing a smile before moving on, her hope waning with each interaction. This was the reaction to each person that said they haven't seen her mother. When they left the store, they went to another store and did the same thing. Both taking each sides of the stores.

As they left the store, Myia felt her phone buzz in her pocket. She quickly pulled it out to see a text from Zara.

"No leads here. How's it going on your end?"

Myia typed back quickly. *"No luck. Just talking to people, but no one has seen her. Meetup at Dan's?"*

After another two hours of no leads, Myia started to feel discouraged. She knew in her heart that something happened but she didn't want Tyson to know. Myia felt her phone buzzed again. She quickly pulled it out to see a text from her aunt.

"The kids are good. I heard from the others too. Keep me posted."

Myia felt a surge of gratitude for her aunt. *"We will. We're about to meet up with them now."*

Just then, Tyson approached, a concerned look on his face. "Any luck?"

"Not really," Myia replied, feeling the weight of disappointment. "But we'll keep trying."

"Let's check in with Marcus and Zara," Tyson suggested, glancing at his watch. "It's almost time."

"Yeah, good idea," Myia agreed. They walked back toward the parking lot, determination etched on their faces. They wouldn't give up; they couldn't.

As they reached the car, Marcus and Zara were already waiting, their expressions mirroring the same mix of hope and frustration.

"Find anything?" Myia asked as they all gathered together.

"Nothing concrete," Marcus replied, running a hand through his hair. "But I spoke to a few people who are going to keep an eye out."

"Same here," Tyson added.

"It's getting late," Zara said. "We should just call Auntie now. She deserves to know we haven't found anything."

Myia nodded, "Yeah, you're right. Besides I'm sure those kids drove her crazy today."

"I just hate telling her we've hit a dead end," Marcus muttered.

"She might have some ideas we haven't thought of," Tyson replied, his voice steady, but the worry in his eyes betrayed him. "She knows mom better than we do."

When they got to Janelle's, they were hit by the rich aroma of spices and roasting vegetables. She was almost finished making dinner and the smells enveloped them like a comforting blanket. Janelle looked up from the stove, her face lighting up at the sight of them. "You're back! Dinner's almost ready.."

"Hey, Nelly," Tyson interrupted gently. "We need to talk."

Her smile faded as she saw the expressions on their faces. "What's wrong?"

Marcus took a deep breath. "We didn't find any leads today and we're all worried"

Her gaze shifted, concern etched into her features. "I am too. Let's sit down. We'll talk about it after dinner."

Myia glanced at her cousins. They hadn't really had a moment to breathe yet. "Sounds good," she replied, forcing a smile.

"Plus, I made your favorite, Myia," Janelle added, stirring the pot. "Shrimp pasta with garlic bread. I thought it might cheer you up. I also made a vegetable tagine for those who want to eat it with me."

Aidyen's eyes lit up. "Yay! Pasta!" He bounced in his seat, and the sight tugged at Myia's heart.

As they dug into dinner, the clinking of forks and the warm chatter of family filled the room. Tyson managed a few jokes, which elicited laughter from Aiyden, making the atmosphere feel lighter, even if only for a moment.

Janelle watched her niece and the others. "You all are doing everything you can. I want you to remember that."

After dinner, as the last bites were cleared away, Janelle wiped her hands on a towel and leaned against the counter. "Alright, let's talk."

The table grew quiet, the weight of their mission settling back in. "I know it's hard to feel like you're not making progress," Janelle began, her voice steady but filled with warmth. "But every little bit counts."

"I think tomorrow we should start early," Tyson suggested. "We can revisit the spots we've already been and check them again thoroughly."

"I agree," Marcus chimed in. "We can split up and cover more ground."

Janelle nodded, but there was a hint of hesitation in her eyes. "That sounds great, but I need to let you know I'll be heading back to work in the morning. I won't be able to join you."

Myia felt a pang of disappointment. "Are you sure? We could really use your support."

Janelle smiled softly, "I know, sweetie, but I've got commitments I can't ignore. I'll be thinking of you all, and I promise to check in during my breaks."

Zara glanced at her aunt, "What if something happens while you're gone?"

"Then you can call me or text me. I will respond and if necessary, I'll leave early."

"We'll be careful," Marcus reassured her. "We'll keep our phones on and stay connected."

The room was heavy with the mix of exhaustion and worry that had settled over them all since the search began. The comforting scent of dinner lingered in the air, but it did little to ease the gnawing anxiety in Myia's chest. They had spent the entire day asking questions, retracing her mother's steps, and checking every corner of the neighborhood. But it felt like they were getting nowhere. The silence that followed Janelle's words seemed to deepen as everyone processed what had just been said.

"We're not giving up," Myia finally spoke, her voice steady despite the turmoil she felt inside. "We've come this far. We'll keep pushing until we find something."

Janelle's eyes softened. "I know, Myia. I know you're all doing your best, but you can't carry this burden alone. You need to take care of yourselves too."

Tyson nodded, his usual light-hardheartedness now absent. "We know, Aunt Nelly. But we can't stop. We just need more time."

The weight of the conversation pressed on her, but Myia forced herself to look at her brother and cousin, seeing the same frustration mirrored in their eyes. The two were already thinking ahead, strategizing, but Myia couldn't shake the sense of urgency that had taken hold of her.

"We'll make a plan tonight," Marcus said, breaking the silence.

Myia glanced at Tyson, who gave her a small, reassuring smile. She knew they both needed sleep more than anything right now, but the thought of waiting felt unbearable. She glanced at her phone again, hoping for any news, any update, but it remained silent.

Janelle's voice broke through her thoughts. "It's late, but I'll be up if you need me. Just keep me posted."

"I'll be up early," Myia said, her voice firm. "Let's meet back here at 7:00. We'll hit it hard tomorrow. No more running around aimlessly. We'll have a plan, and we'll stick to it."

Tyson stretched in his chair, then stood. "I'm with you."

—-

Later that night, Myia lay in her bed, her eyes wide open as she stared at the ceiling. Sleep felt distant and fleeting, like a luxury she couldn't afford. The house was quiet, save for the soft hum of the air conditioning. The thoughts kept swirling in her mind: *What had happened to her mom? Where was she? Why hadn't she come home yet?* Every question only made the fear and doubt inside her grow.

Her phone buzzed again, interrupting her thoughts. It was a message from Marcus.

"*I'm going to be up for a bit. If you need anything, let me know.*"

She stared at the message for a moment, grateful for his offer. She quickly typed back.

"*Thanks. I'm good. Just thinking.*"

"*I get it. We'll figure this out. Just try to rest.*"

Myia sighed and tossed the phone to the side, sitting up in bed. Her mind wouldn't stop racing, but she knew she had to find a way to calm herself before tomorrow. The silence of the house felt so foreign, so loud in her ears. It was almost too much to bear. She thought back to the mornings when her mom was there, when everything was simple, when she'd find comfort in hearing her mom's voice or seeing her smile.

Now, all she had was this unbearable quiet. She didn't know how long she laid there before she heard Tyson's voice at the door. He had his hand resting on the frame, his face serious but soft.

"You okay?" he asked quietly, his voice barely above a whisper.

Myia swallowed the lump in her throat, but nodded. "Just can't sleep. My mind won't shut off."

Tyson walked into the room and sat down on the edge of her bed, his presence a steady, grounding force. "I know. Same here. But we'll figure it out, Myia. We will." She was thankful for her brother. He had always been her rock, the one she could rely on, and right now, his calm demeanor was the only thing keeping her from unraveling.

"I know," she said quietly. "But I just keep thinking... what if we don't find her?"

Tyson didn't hesitate. "We will. We've got people out there looking for her, we've got eyes everywhere. It's just gonna take time, that's all. And we're not stopping. We're gonna find her, Myia. I swear." Tyson gave her a small smile before standing up.

"Get some sleep. I'll be up in the morning. We'll hit it again first thing."

Myia was grateful for his words, even though she wasn't sure if she'd sleep at all.

"Thanks, Ty," she said, her voice thick with emotion.

He paused at the door and glanced back at her, offering one last reassuring look before disappearing into the hall. Myia lay back down, staring at the ceiling once more, trying to steady her breathing. In the darkness, she made a promise to herself, and to her mother, that she wouldn't stop searching. No matter how long it took.

Chapter 18

It's been five days since Niyah's disappearance. The news had spread quickly through the city. Posters with her face had been plastered across town. Volunteers had flooded the streets, combing through parks, alleyways, and abandoned lots. Social media had exploded with pleas for information. But as each day passed, hope began to dwindle, replaced by a slow-growing dread.

Isaac Whitmore, a city worker who had spent more than two decades maintaining the parks, was on his rounds that Thursday afternoon. Normally, the approach of Labor Day was one of his favorite times of the year. The trees would be full and green, the lawns freshly mowed, and the laughter of children would echo through the park as they played on the swings or chased each other through the fields. But today, the park was quiet, too quiet for late August.

Isaac had started his day like any other, with a thermos of coffee in hand and a mental checklist of tasks to complete. He made his way through the park, clearing debris, trimming overgrown shrubs, and ensuring the grounds were ready for the weekend's upcoming events. The familiar tasks usually calmed his mind, but today, his thoughts were elsewhere.

He couldn't stop thinking about her. He had never met her personally, but everyone knew about her now. The story had been all over the news, and Isaac couldn't help but feel the weight of it. His daughters were about her age, and the thought of someone so young, so vibrant, disappearing without a trace sent chills down his spine. He'd heard that volunteers had already searched through Hidden Oaks, but Isaac couldn't shake the feeling that something was off. As he raked leaves along one of the quieter paths tucked behind a grove of oak trees, a knot of unease twisted in his stomach.

The pile of leaves in front of him was larger than normal. It hadn't rained recently, and the leaves, though sparse, seemed to have gathered unnaturally in this one spot. Isaac hesitated, his hands gripping the rake. The sun was high in the sky, casting long shadows through the trees, but the area seemed to hold an unusual stillness. He pushed the rake through the pile, expecting the satisfying scrape of leaves against earth.

But something wasn't right. Beneath the leaves, the ground felt different. It wasn't just dirt and foliage. His rake hit something soft, something that shouldn't have been there. His breath caught, and a cold sweat broke out across his forehead. His heart pounded in his chest as he knelt down, pushing the leaves aside with his hands.

It was then that he saw it. A glimpse of something unnatural; fabric, a patterned material that didn't belong in the sea of brown and gold leaves. His heart hammered in his chest, and for a moment, he couldn't move. He dropped the rake, his hands suddenly trembled as he knelt down for a closer look.

There, just beneath the surface of the leaves, was the unmistakable outline of a body. The fabric he saw was animal print, a shirt. His breath caught as he pulled away some of the leaves, revealing more: a tattooed arm, black pants that were caked with dirt, bright blonde lemonade braids,and one animal print shoe.

Isaac staggered back, his hand flying to his mouth as the horror of what he had just uncovered hit him all at once. He knew exactly who she was. This was the young woman who had disappeared without a trace. Her family had begged for information, pleaded with the public to help bring her home. He stumbled backwards as he struggled to pull his phone from his pocket.His hands shook as he pulled out his phone, dialing 911. His breath came in shallow gasps as the line rings, his mind racing, praying that this isn't real, that he's just seeing things. But the familiar figure, the hair, the outfit, everything about the body screamed Niyah. He pressed the phone to his ear, trying to steady himself.

"911, what's your emergency?"

"This is Isaac Whitmore. I... I think I..." Isaac stammered, struggling to find the words. He took a deep breath, his voice breaking as he continued. "I found a body. I... I think it might be that missing woman. Niyah Thompson."

There was a pause on the other end before the operator spoke again, her tone steady. "Sir, can you tell me your location?"

"I... I'm at Hidden Oaks Park near the back entrance. Please, you need to send someone out here. I... I'm not sure what to do."

"Stay on the line with me, sir," the operator instructed. "Help is on the way. Can you tell me if the person is breathing or if there are any signs of life?"

"No... no, I don't think so. She's... she's not moving."

The operator's voice remained calm, grounding him. "Okay, sir. Don't touch anything. Just stay where you are and wait for the authorities. They'll be there shortly."

"Alright," he whispered. His eyes were drawn back to that scene. Her bright blonde braids were matted with dirt and her small black cross body purse lay partially hidden beneath her. It looked untouched, as though it had been gently placed there, not thrown or discarded.

Time seemed to blur after that. The minutes felt like hours as he waited, pacing in small, frantic circles. The once-peaceful park now seemed to loom over him, the trees that had earlier whispered in the wind now felt like silent witnesses to something terrible. He kept his distance from the body, afraid to look, but unable to fully turn away. The silence was suffocating.

For a moment, his mind spiraled. *How had she ended up here? Hidden Oaks was so far from where she'd last been seen, miles from her home. Had someone dumped her body here, thinking no one would ever find it?* His gut churned with the thought. There had to be answers, but none of them came to him now.

He heard the sound of sirens in the distance, growing closer. His breath came in ragged gasps as the first police car pulled into the gravel lot. Detective Samuels, a seasoned officer who had been working the missing person's case, and his team arrived quickly, the atmosphere instantly shifting as they moved with purpose, their faces grim.

"Step back," Samuels instructed gently, placed a hand on Isaac's shoulder. "We'll take it from here." Isaac backed away as the officers and crime scene investigators took over. They worked swiftly and secured the area. The officers were speaking low as they knelt by the body. It wasn't long before the entire park seemed to be swarmed by law enforcement, yellow tape cutting through the quiet landscape. It was a grim reminder of the reality that had settled in.

Samuels crouched near the body, his face tightening as he took in the sight of her lifeless form. "Damn it," he muttered under his breath. His mind started to piece through the details. This wasn't how it was supposed to end. They had hoped to find her alive, to bring her back to her family. But now, all they could do was try to give her family closure and find whoever had done this.

Isaac stood at the edge of the scene, trying to mentally process what was happening at that moment. He watched helplessly as Detective Samuels and his team began their work. His mind raced, replaying everything he had seen that morning. The body, lifeless and abandoned, hidden among the trees of Hidden Oaks. Niyah... his heart twisted with her name. He couldn't fathom how it had come to this. He could already imagine the devastation her family would feel when they learned the truth.

Detective Samuels stood up, wiping his gloved hands together, his face grim and worn. "Mr. Whitmore," he said, his voice rough with exhaustion. "You did the right thing by coming forward. But I need you to step aside while we process the scene. I'll need a statement from you later. Just... let us handle it from here."

Isaac nodded mutely, too numb to argue. Samuels' words barely registered as he stepped back, still caught in a haze of shock. He couldn't look away from the body, from the way the yellow tape flapped in the wind, marking off a crime scene where the unthinkable had happened.

Chapter 19

Isaac stood at a distance, his arms crossed tightly against his chest. The once familiar surroundings of Hidden Oaks Park now felt like a crime scene etched in his memory. He had been here countless times, fixing benches, cleaning trails, and removing trash, but today, the park was filled with flashing lights, police tape, and hushed conversations that carried a weight far heavier than fallen leaves.

The officers moved efficiently, marking off areas, taking photographs, and collecting evidence. They wore somber expressions, each one carrying the same sense of urgency Isaac felt in his bones. He watched as detectives crouched near the pile of leaves, now cleared away to reveal the resting place of Niyah Thompson. The medics stood nearby, waiting with the stretcher, their faces set in professional detachment. Isaac couldn't shake the image of her face from his mind. The look of peace that somehow seemed wrong given the circumstances.

He shifted his weight from one foot to the other, trying to stay out of the way but unable to pull himself away from the scene. He had given his statement, telling them everything he knew, but it didn't feel like enough. Isaac kept wondering if there was something he had missed, something he should have seen or done differently.

Detective Samuels was speaking with a forensic technician when he glanced up and caught Isaac's eye. He walked over, his face a blend of weariness and professionalism. Isaac had a feeling the detective had seen many scenes like this before, but the lines on his face suggested that this one was taking its toll.

"Mr. Whitmore?" Samuels asked, his voice low and steady.

Isaac nodded, swallowing the lump in his throat. "Yeah."

"We appreciate you staying here," Samuels said. "I know this isn't easy."

Isaac rubbed the back of his neck, trying to ease the tension building there. "It's just... I feel like I should be doing more, you know? I was the one who found her. I..." He trailed off, shaking his head. The words seemed so inadequate.

"You've done more than enough. Finding her and calling us right away was the best thing you could have done."

"But it doesn't feel like enough," Isaac muttered. He took a deep breath, trying to shake the weight that seemed to press down on his chest. He didn't know her personally, but now he felt connected to her in a way he couldn't explain. He had been the one to find her, and for him it was a heavy burden to carry.

"What happens next?" Isaac asked, almost dreading the answer.

Samuels sighed, his expression turning grim. "We have to complete the scene investigation. Forensics will collect evidence, and then we'll move her body. We'll be reaching out to her family soon."

Isaac nodded slowly. He glanced over at the officers who were carefully marking the area where her body was found. It seemed so sterile, so mechanical, and yet he knew it was necessary. These people had a job to do, one that would hopefully lead to answers and, eventually, to justice.

"Is there... any idea what happened?" Isaac asked hesitantly.

"We're still figuring that out," Samuels answered. "But it's clear this wasn't an accident."

Isaac's stomach tightened at the confirmation of what he had suspected. He hadn't known how she had died, but there was something unsettling about the way she had been left there, hidden beneath the leaves as if someone had wanted her to stay lost. The thought gnawed at him, a cold shiver running down his spine. Whoever had done this had taken deliberate steps to ensure she wasn't found, at least not easily. The quiet, almost deliberate way her body had been concealed in the underbrush felt like a message. One Isaac couldn't yet understand, but it made his skin crawl. He glanced around, as if expecting the answers to jump out from the trees or the shadows, but there was nothing. Just the stillness of the trees, watching him back.

"Listen," Samuels continued, his tone gentler, "you've been through a lot today. You should go home, try to get some rest. We'll be in touch if we have more questions."

Isaac nodded, though he couldn't imagine resting any time soon. He felt like there was a knot in his chest that wouldn't untangle. But he also knew there wasn't anything more he could do here. The professionals were on it now.

Before leaving, Isaac turned back for one last look at the park. He had always loved the way Hidden Oaks felt like an escape from the rest of the world, a place of peace and quiet. But now, that sense of tranquility had been shattered. He couldn't imagine ever walking these trails again without thinking of what happened today.

As he walked to his truck, Isaac felt his pocket vibrate. He pulled it his phone to read a text from his wife:

"Dinner's ready when you are. You okay?"

He stared at the message, trying to figure out how to respond. He didn't want to burden her with what he had seen, but he also didn't want to lie. So he typed a simple reply:

"Not really. But I'll be home soon."

He climbed into the truck and sat there for a moment, gripping the steering wheel tightly as he tried to steady his breathing. Isaac had always been good at compartmentalizing, at pushing the tough stuff aside to get through the day. But this wasn't something he could just shove into a box and ignore. He knew he would carry this day with him for a long time.

Taking one last look in the rear view mirror, he saw the blue and red lights reflecting off the trees, flickering like distorted fireflies in the growing twilight. He took a deep breath and turned the key, the truck's engine roaring to life. As he pulled away from the park, he couldn't help but feel like he was leaving something behind.

He pulled into his driveway and cut the engine, the sudden silence of the truck feeling almost too loud. For a moment, he just sat there, staring at the house in front of him, thinking about how everything had changed in the last few hours. He had left for work that morning with no idea that by the end of the day, he would be a witness to a crime, a tragedy that would alter the course of a family's life.

Chapter 20

Detective Samuels pulled into the driveway of Niyah's house, turning off the engine of his unmarked cruiser. He sat there for a moment, letting the silence envelop him as he stared at the house before him. It was the kind of suburban home you'd drive past without thinking twice, modest, with a well-tended lawn and a porch that spoke of countless family gatherings. But tonight, this house would become a place marked by grief, forever linked to the memory of unimaginable loss.

He sighed, running a hand over his face. This was always the hardest part. His mind cycled through the right words to say, as if there were such a thing in moments like these. He could see the lights on inside, shadows moving past the windows. They were home. He wasn't sure whether that was a good thing or a bad thing. At least they wouldn't be receiving this news alone.

"Here we go," he muttered to himself, opening the car door. Stepping out, he felt the evening chill seep through his coat. He adjusted his badge to be more visible and approached the front door with careful, deliberate steps. He could hear faint voices inside. It sounded like muffled conversations. He also heard the creak of a floorboard. He took a deep breath as he raised his hand to knock.

It was Marcus who answered the door. He looked exhausted, his face drawn and eyes rimmed red, the stress of the past few days etched deeply into his features. He opened the door wider when he saw the detective. "Can I help you?" Marcus's voice was tight, guarded.

Samuels took a deep breath. "My name is Detective Samuels with Crest Ridge Missing Persons'. Can I come in?" Marcus stepped back to let the detective in. Samuels followed him into the living room, where the rest of the family was gathered. Myia, Tyson, and Zara looked up as the detective entered, their tired faces instantly sharpening with fear. They all knew that an unannounced visit from the police at this hour could only mean one thing.

Samuels cleared his throat, trying to maintain his professional demeanor. He knew there was no easy way to deliver news like this. He had done it dozens of times, and it never got any easier. "I'm Detective Samuels," he began, keeping his voice steady and calm. "I'm very sorry to have to tell you this, but your mom's body was found earlier today."

Time seemed to stop for a moment, the air in the room turning heavy and suffocating. Myia felt the room tilt around her, her breath caught in her throat. Zara's hand flew to her mouth, tears instantly welling up. Tyson leaned forward in his chair, as if trying to make sense of the words. He refused to accept what they meant.

"What?" Myia's voice came out in a strangled whisper, barely audible. "You... you found her?"

"Yes, we did. I'm so sorry. We found her in Hidden Oaks Park earlier today."

"No..." Myia whispered as she stumbled forward. She clung to Zara, her sobs quiet at first, then growing louder, more desperate. "No, no, no..."

Tyson stood up, his fists clenched tightly at his sides. Anger, disbelief, and sorrow warred for control on his face. He shook his head, his voice barely more than a growl. "Who did this? Who did this to her?"

"We're still investigating," Samuels replied, his voice soft. "Right now, we're working to determine what happened and who's responsible."

Marcus remained standing, staring blankly at the floor. The room was filled with the sounds of quiet sobs and shuddered breaths. It was as if the world had shattered around them, and all that remained were the jagged pieces of their lives, scattered and irreparable. TZara, who had been holding it together for Myia's sake, finally broke down. She hugged Myia tightly, both of them crying into each other's shoulders. Tyson stood up abruptly, pacing back and forth as if he could outrun the emotions threatening to overwhelm him.

Samuels gave them a moment before speaking again. "I know this is incredibly difficult to hear, and I'm so sorry that you have to go through this," he said gently. "We'll be working day and night to find out who did this. I promise you that."

Marcus finally looked up, meeting the detective's gaze. His voice was low, almost defeated. "How did she... how did she die?"

"We're still waiting for the medical examiner's report," Samuels replied carefully, not wanting to overwhelm them with too many details just yet. "Right now, we're focusing on gathering evidence and tracking down leads."

The room fell into silence once more. The clock on the wall ticked loudly, marking each passing second as the weight of reality settled in. Myia wiped her tears away with the back of her hand, trying to catch her breath.

"What do we do now?" she asked, her voice barely audible.

"For now, you just focus on taking care of each other," Samuels advised softly. "We'll keep you informed of any developments in the investigation. And if you think of anything, anything at all that might help, please don't hesitate to call me."

He handed Marcus his card, "My direct number is printed on the back." It felt like a small, insignificant thing to give them in the face of such overwhelming loss, but it was all he could offer right now.

"Thank you," he said quietly, tucking the card into his pocket. He still felt numb, as if he were moving through a fog, disconnected from reality.

Samuels glanced around at the family, each of them dealing with the news in their own way. He had seen this before, different people, different families, but always the same heart-wrenching grief. And it never got any easier to watch.

"If there's anything else I can do," he began, but his words trailed off as he realized there was nothing he could say that would make this any easier. He stood there for a moment, unsure of what else to do, then nodded once more and quietly made his way to the door. He paused, looking back at the family huddled together, trying to offer each other the comfort they desperately needed.

Detective Samuels closed the door softly behind him, walking back to his cruiser with the weight of the world on his shoulders. He knew this was only the beginning of a long, painful journey for her family. And he couldn't shake the feeling that he had somehow failed them, that finding her body wasn't enough. It wouldn't bring her back, and it wouldn't heal the wounds left behind. He knew the only things that could make up for all of this is to find out what had happened to her. If he could do that, then it would bring her family some semblance of justice.

After he left, the silence in the house was deafening. It felt like a vacuum had sucked all the air out of the room. The four cousins were left to grapple with the weight of what had just been said, trying to piece together some semblance of reality from the shattered fragments left behind.

Zara let out a shaky breath and pulled Myia into a tighter hug. Tyson, who had been pacing anxiously, finally slumped into a chair, burying his face in his hands. Marcus stood in the corner, staring blankly at the wall as if it could give him the answers he so desperately sought. It was Myia who finally broke the silence. "We... we need to call Auntie," she murmured, her voice barely more than a whisper.

The mention of Janelle's name was like a jolt of electricity through the room. All eyes turned to Myia, but no one spoke. They were all thinking the same thing: How were they going to tell her?

Zara sniffed, wiping at her eyes with the back of her hand. "We can't just... let her find out on her own," she said, her voice trembling. "We have to tell her before she hears it from someone else."

Tyson looked up. "But who's going to do it?" he asked, his voice strained. "Who's going to break her heart like that?"

It was a question none of them wanted to answer. Janelle had been holding onto hope, clinging to the belief that her sister was still out there alive. She had been the one who reassured everyone, who organized the family's efforts to search, who kept the faith even when the rest of them were falling apart.

Myia felt her stomach twist with dread. Her aunt had been the glue holding the family together these past five days, but Myia knew that glue would come undone with just a few words. And yet, someone had to do it. Someone had to bear that awful responsibility.

"I'll call her," Myia said, her voice barely audible.

Zara looked at her, wide-eyed. "Are you sure?" she asked softly. "You don't have to—"

"No," Myia interrupted, her voice steady despite the tears welling in her eyes. "I have to. She deserves to hear it from me."

Chapter 21

Janelle was sitting at her desk, trying to focus on the spreadsheet in front of her. The numbers blurred together, and her fingers idly tapped the keys without much thought. She had been working from home for days, but focusing had been nearly impossible. Every time her phone buzzed, she found herself holding her breath, hoping it was news about her sister.

She had been pacing through her living room, kitchen, and even the back porch, trying to keep her mind from racing too far down the path of what-ifs and worst-case scenarios. Darren was supposed to be coming home soon from work, and she had planned to go out to dinner and try to figure out what their next move was. Even though the search efforts continued and the police kept saying they were doing everything they could, it was hard to keep her hope intact when every call brought more waiting.

She sighed heavily, taking off her glasses and rubbing her temples. That's when her phone rang. She looked down and saw Myia's name flashing on the screen. Her heart immediately lurched into her throat. "Hey, sweetie," she said, attempting to sound casual. But there was a tension there, a silent plea for good news.

"Nelly ...." she paused, as if struggling to get the words out.

Janelle's pulse quickened. She couldn't explain it, but she felt something was wrong. It was the way Myia said her name, the way she seemed to choke on the words. "Myia?" Janelle's voice wavered, a tremor she couldn't conceal. "What happened? Did the police find something?"

Myia's silence stretched for what felt like an eternity. And then, softly, she said the words Janelle had been dreading. "They found her. They found Mom," Myia choked out, her voice raw with pain. "She's... gone."

"No," Janelle whispered, shaking her head as if Myia could see her through the phone. "No, that's not true... That can't be true." Her voice broke, and she clutched at her chest, trying to hold back the panic that was rising within her.

"I'm so sorry," Myia whispered, her voice barely audible through her tears.

Janelle felt her knees buckle, and she sank to the floor, her hand still gripping the phone. Her breath came in shallow gasps, and the room seemed to spin around her. She could hear Darren's voice calling her name, asking what was wrong, but it sounded distant, like he was speaking through water.

Her voice broke, and her body shook as the sobs overtook her. Her sister, the one she had grown up with, laughed with, fought with gone. It didn't make sense. It couldn't be real. She couldn't be gone. This was all some horrible nightmare, and she was going to wake up any second now.

But Myia's voice was real, and the pain in her words was unmistakable. "Nelly... I'm so sorry," she repeated, her own voice breaking.

Janelle couldn't speak. She felt like she was drowning, the grief pulling her under, suffocating her. Darren was beside her now, his hands on her shoulders, shaking her gently. "Baby," he said, his voice frantic. "Baby, what happened?"

She couldn't speak, couldn't explain. All she could do was sob into his chest, the phone falling from her hand, Myia's broken voice still faintly audible on the other end. Darren reached for the phone, taking it from her trembling hand.

"Myia, what's going on?" Darren demanded, his voice shaking with a mix of fear and urgency.

Myia's words were barely a whisper. "They found my mom. She... she's gone."

Darren let out a long, shaky breath. He glanced down at his wife, who was still curled up on the floor crying uncontrollable. He closed his eyes, trying to steady himself. "We'll be there soon," he managed to say before hanging up the phone.

He turned back to Janelle, gently pulling her into his arms. She clung to him, her cries muffled against his chest. He held her tightly, trying to be strong for both of them, but he felt like the ground had just crumbled beneath him.

After what felt like an eternity, Janelle's sobs began to quiet, and she pulled back slightly, looking up at Darren with red, tear-stained eyes. "We... we have to go," she whispered. "We have to be there... for Myia and Tyson. They need us."

Darren nodded. "I'll drive." He kissed her forehead, his own heart aching for her, for her family. But before they could leave, there were a few more calls she had to make.

She stared at her phone, the screen still smudged with tears, and her heart sank at the thought of what she had to do next. Their parents, who were divorced, would be devastated by the news. She didn't know how she would find the strength to tell them.

She dialed her mother's number first. The phone rang once... twice... three times before her mother's familiar voice answered, full of warmth and hope. "Hey, Janie. Any news? Did they find her?"

Janelle's breath hitched in her throat. The words felt heavy, impossible to say. "Mom... they found her. But she's... she's gone. Niyah's gone."

There was a long, awful silence on the other end of the line. She held her breath, waiting, her stomach churning as the silence stretched on. Then, suddenly, there was a click.

Her mother had hung up.

Janelle stared at the phone in disbelief, her heart shattering all over again. Her mother had simply hung up. As if by ending the call, she could end the reality of the news. As if not hearing it meant it wasn't true.

She wanted to scream, to throw the phone across the room, to do anything to release the anguish that filled her chest. But she didn't. She couldn't.

Instead, with trembling fingers, she dialed her father's number. Her father's voice was slower, tired, and filled with a kind of quiet hope that made her chest ache even more. "Hey, darling daughter. What's going on?" Janelle swallowed the lump in her throat, her voice breaking as she spoke. "Dad... they found her. They found Niyah. It's just us now."

The silence that followed wasn't as long this time, but it was just as painful. She could hear her father's breath catch on the other end, the faint tremble in his voice as he processed the news.

"No..." he whispered, his voice barely audible. "Not my girl. Not Niyah..."

She bit her lip, trying to hold back the fresh wave of tears that threatened to spill over. "I'm so sorry, Dad. I'm so sorry."

Then, for the first time in her life, she heard her father cry. His sobs were quiet, soft, the kind of deep, soul-wrenching grief that comes from losing something irreplaceable. She had never heard her father cry like that before, and the sound of it broke her heart all over again.

After a few minutes, he composed himself enough to speak. "I... I can't believe it," he whispered. "She was so full of life. She was..." His voice trailed off, too overcome with emotion to continue.

"I know, Dad," Janelle whispered, her voice thick with tears. "I know. We're going over to Myia's house now. They need us."

"I'll be there soon," he said, his voice cracking. "I need to... I need to process this. But I'll be there."

She hung up, her heart heavy, but the worst wasn't over yet. She thought of Jordan, who had been working long hours and was likely fast asleep, getting his rest for his next shift. He didn't know yet.

Her hands shook as she dialed his number, knowing she had to wake him with the news no mother ever wants to deliver. The phone rang for several moments, each second more agonizing than the last. Finally, his groggy voice answered.

"Hey, Mom," he mumbled, still half-asleep. "What's going on?"

Her breath hitched again, and she struggled to keep her voice steady. "Jordan... it's about your Aunt ."

The pause on the other end was immediate, and she could almost hear him sitting up in bed, alert now. "What is it? Did they find her?"

Her voice trembled. "Yes they found her, ... but she's gone. Your aunt is gone."

There was a sharp intake of breath from Jordan, followed by a long silence. She knew he was processing, trying to grasp the words that had just shattered their world. He had always been close to his aunt, her energy, her warmth had drawn him in just like everyone else in the family.

"No..." His voice was thick with disbelief. "No, that can't be right, Mom. Are you sure?"

Her heart broke all over again. "I'm so sorry, baby. The police... they confirmed it. We're going over to Myia's now. We all need to be together."

He didn't speak for a long time, but she could hear the soft sound of his breathing. Finally, he whispered, "I'll meet you there."

Janelle hung up, and for a moment, she simply sat there, the weight of the calls she had made pressing down on her like a tidal wave. Darren was there, his arms wrapping around her as she broke down once more. "It's going to be okay," he murmured, though he didn't know if it was true. "We'll get through this.

Janelle nodded, though she wasn't sure if she believed it. All she knew was that she had to keep moving, keep going, for the sake of her family.

They left the house in silence, the weight of their grief hanging heavily between them. The drive to Myia's house felt like a blur, the world outside the car seeming unreal, disconnected from the pain that was consuming them both.

When they arrived, Janelle saw Marcus, Tyson, and Zara waiting on the porch, their faces etched with grief. Myia stood in the doorway, her eyes red and swollen from crying. When she saw her aunt, she ran towards her.

"I'm so sorry, Auntie," Myia sobbed, her voice breaking.

Janelle held her tightly, her own tears spilling over once more. "It's not your fault, Myia," she whispered, her voice trembling. "It's not your fault..."

Chapter 22

Kelly Crenshaw had just finished her shift at The Crimson Manor. Her body ached from the constant rush of orders, the clattering of dishes, and the chaos of a busy night. She walked in her apartment and dropped onto her couch, too exhausted to even think about changing out of her uniform. After a long night like tonight, all she wanted to do was sink into the comfort of her couch and zone out.

She flicked on the TV, hoping for something mindless to drown out the exhaustion. But instead, the local news grabbed her attention. The headline that flashed across the screen made her sit up straight:

"Body Found in Hidden Oaks Identified as Niyah Thompson."

Her breath caught in her throat as the anchor continued, *"A body discovered today in Hidden Oaks Park has been identified as Niyah Thompson who had been missing since Last Saturday. She was last seen leaving an apartment building. Authorities are investigating the case as a homicide and are urging anyone with information about her last known whereabouts to come forward."*

Kelly froze, her eyes snapping to the screen. There was the face of the woman she had served just a few nights ago. She had been in the restaurant and sat at one of Kelly's tables. A surge of cold dread washed over her as the details came back, clear as day. Niyah had been with a man that looked familiar, but she had the hardest time trying to remember his name. Then it all came to her. His name was Malik. Malik Johnson. He was a regular there.

Her heart pounded in her chest as the scene played out again in her mind. Malik had been coming to the restaurant for months. He wasn't a daily customer, but he showed up often enough. Always polite, always composed, and always paid in cash. He would meet a different person each time he came.

But this time had been different. She had waited on him and his date. She checked on them constantly, but when he asked for the check, his behavior changed, and in her opinion, became unsettling. The smile on his face had vanished, replaced by something more guarded. His eyes, once charming and warm, now looked cold and calculating. His posture stiffened as he fumbled with his wallet, almost too carefully, and for a split second, Kelly thought she saw him glance over his shoulder. It was subtle, but the feeling lingered. She had picked up on it immediately, due to years of experience as a server. At the time, it hadn't seemed all that strange, but now, knowing what had happened, Kelly wished she could have said or done something.

She knew then that she had to call the hotline number. Kelly hesitated for a moment when the person answered, "I think I have information about the woman that was found in the park. She was at my restaurant a few nights ago, The Crimson Manor. I served her and the man she was with. His name is Malik Johnson. He's a regular."

"Thank you for calling. Can you describe him?"

"Yes. He's dark skinned, tall, around six feet. He was wearing a navy blue shirt that night with some dark denim jeans."

"You said he's a regular at the restaurant?"

"Yes," Kelly confirmed. "He comes in pretty often."

"Do you recall what time they left? Or anything unusual?"

"They left around 12:30."

"You did the right thing by calling," the man reassured her. "This information is very important. An officer will contact you shortly to get more details. Can you stay by the phone?"

"Yes, I'll stay."

As she waited, the guilt settled in her mind. She felt that something wasn't right, and yet she had done nothing. *"Why hadn't she said something? Why hadn't she trusted her gut?"* The loud ringtone of her phone startled her.

"Hello?" Kelly answered.

"Hi, is this Miss Crenshaw?" the voice on the other end asked.

"Yes, this is she."

"This is Officer Harris. I understand you have information about the missing woman."

The mention of Niyah's name sent a chill through Kelly. She gripped the phone tighter, forcing herself to focus. "Yes... I..I think I might have seen her with someone... someone suspicious." Her voice wavered, but she pressed on. "I think I might have missed something important. I didn't act fast enough." Her stomach churned as the weight of the situation pressed down on her. The officer's voice cut through the fog of her thoughts.

"That's exactly why we need you to walk us through everything you remember. Every detail counts."

"I can do that."

"Can you tell me what time did they leave?"

"Around 12:30. They left together."

"Did you overhear any part of their conversation?"

"I only caught the last part when they asked for the check. She said she wanted to go home and he didn't look to happy to hear that."

"This is very helpful. We'll be in touch soon, but please stay available in case we need to ask more questions."

After hanging up, Kelly sat in stunned silence. She had done what she could, given the police everything that she remembered. But it didn't feel like enough. Malik was a regular customer. Now, the thought of him made her stomach turn.

Officer Harris sat at his desk, staring at the notes he had just taken from his conversation with Kelly. The lead she provided was invaluable. It's pointing to Malik Johnson and that he was possibly the last person seen with Niyah. His gut told him they were onto something big. Without wasting any time, Harris picked up the phone and dialed Detective Samuels, his direct superior in the homicide unit.

Samuels picked up the phone. "Harris, what've you got?"

Harris didn't waste time. "Detective, I just got off the line with a woman named Kelly Crenshaw who works over at The Crimson Manor. She called in to give a tip about the suspect in the Niyah Thompson case."

Samuels immediately straightened in his chair. "Go on," he urged, trying to keep his voice steady.

"Kelly said she recognized him from the restaurant. She told me that he was with Niyah the night she went missing."

"Did she mention a name?"

" Yes, Malik Johnson. And that he's a regular."

Samuels, always quick to act on solid information, didn't hesitate. "Good work, Harris. This information changes everything. If he's involved with Niyah's disappearance and death, we need him in custody now."

Harris could hear papers rustling on Samuels' end as he prepared to escalate the situation. "I'll put out an APB on him right away," Samuels said, his voice growing more urgent. "We can't afford to let him slip away, especially if he knows we're onto him. Contact the rest of the team. I want patrol cars scouring the area. He's probably still in the city, which means someone's bound to have seen him recently."

"Understood, sir," Harris repl.

Hanging up, Samuels wasted no time, alerting every law enforcement officer in the city. He gave a detailed description based on what Kelly had provided. With the APB now out, patrol units would be on high alert, and Malik's image would be blasted to every available officer.

Samuels leaned back in his chair, his mind already racing with possibilities. Malik Johnson wasn't just some random name anymore. He was their prime suspect. And now, with the entire city watching for him, it was only a matter of time before Malik was found.

Chapter 23

Detective Samuels took a deep breath before picking up his phone. He scrolled through his notes, finding Myia's number. The family had been through so much already, but he needed to fill in the gaps with their help. Myia had been cooperative during previous conversations, but this time he needed to tread carefully. He couldn't risk making the situation any harder on her.

The phone rang twice before a tired voice answered. "Hello?"

"Myia, it's Detective Samuels," he said, his voice steady but gentle. "I'm sorry to call you like this, but I need some information from you if you're up to it."

"Okay," she replied feeling hopeful.

"We've identified the man who was with your mother that night. His name is Malik Johnson. Does that ring a bell?"

Myia's heart sank. She had heard the name before. Suddenly, everything clicked into place, and she remembered what her mother had mentioned, though never in much detail

"My mom met him online," she said, her voice steady but quiet. "She never told us his last name, but they had been texting and video calling for weeks. That day, at my cousin's place, was the first time she actually met him in person."

Detective Samuels was silent for a moment, absorbing this new information. "So, that was the first time they met in person?"

"Yeah," Myia confirmed. "She didn't tell us anything about him other than she'd been talking to someone. I never knew his name until now."

Marcus, who had been sitting nearby, suddenly looked up. "Wait, Malik? That guy your mom went downstairs to meet?"

Myia nodded. "Yeah. Remember he picked her up at Zara's place the other day? He texted her when he got there, and she went downstairs."

Marcus's eyes widened. "I know the car he drives! It was that SUV that was playing the loud music! I took a picture of it."

"You did?" Myia asked, her pulse quickening.

"Yeah," he said, pulling out his phone and scrolling through his photos. "I went out on the balcony while Mom and Auntie were talking."

"Do you still have that picture?" Detective Samuels asked, his tone sharpening.

"Yeah, I do," Marcus said.

"Text that to me as soon as you can," Detective Samuels said. "My number is on the card I gave you."

"Is there... anything else you need?" Myia asked, and Samuels could hear the exhaustion in her voice.

"Not right now," he said. "If anything comes up, I'll let you know. And if you think of anything else, please don't hesitate to call me, okay?"

"Okay," Myia murmured. "Thanks, Detective."

The call ended, leaving the cousins in a thick silence. Myia stared at the image on Marcus's phone, her mind racing. Her mother had trusted this man, even though she hadn't known him for long. Now, Malik Johnson was the key to unlocking the mystery of what happened in her final hours.

"What do we do now?" Myia asked, her voice shaky.

"We wait for the detective," he said, his jaw tight. "But I'm not waiting long. We need answers."

Myia nodded, her heart heavy with fear and confusion. Malik Johnson wasn't just some random person anymore. He had been woven into their lives, even if only briefly. And now, he held the answers they desperately needed.

Marcus paced around the room, his mind still reeling from the conversation with Detective Samuels. Without thinking, he pulled out his phone and dialed his mom. She answered after a couple of rings, her voice full of concern.

"What's going on?" she asked.

"Mom, you won't believe this," he said, his voice strained. "The detective just called. They've identified the guy who was with Auntie the night she disappeared. His name's Malik Johnson."

There was a brief silence on the other end of the line. "Malik Johnson? I don't know that name," his mom said, confused.

"Neither did we," he continued. "Turns out, Auntie met him online. She'd been talking to him for weeks but didn't meet him in person until that Saturday."

"Oh my God," his mom whispered. "Son, that's... that's unbelievable."

"Yeah, but there's more," he said, his pacing quickening. "Remember when you and Auntie were talking? Well I went to the balcony and took a picture of his ride. I just sent it to the detective."

"It's a good thing you did. That photo could be the key to figuring out what happened to your aunt."

"I didn't even realize how important it would be," he admitted. "But now, I'm glad I did."

"You did the right thing, honey. That photo could lead them to some answers. I'm proud of you.

"Thanks, Mom," he said, his heart heavy but grateful for her words. He heard the deep sigh on the other end of the line, knowing what she was about to say next.

"I need to call Grandma and Grandpa," she said, her voice suddenly more serious. "They need to know what's going on."

"Okay. I'll let you know if we hear anything else from the detective."

"Yeah, you should tell them. Let me know how they take it."

"I will," she said softly. "Talk to you soon."

Janelle ended the call and stared at her phone, her mind whirling with the weight of the news. She took a deep breath and dialed her mother first.

"Mom," she said when her mother answered. "I need to tell you something. There's been an update in Niyah's case."

Her mother's voice trembled on the other end. "What is it, Nelly?"

"The detective got a name. Malik Johnson. And Marcus took a picture of his car."

"So, this Malik is... responsible?"

"We don't know yet but the police are looking into him."

There was a long pause, and then the sound of muffled sobs. "I just... I can't believe this is happening."

"I know, Mom," she said. "I'll keep you updated."

After ending the call, sh dialed her father's number next.

"Hey, Dad," she began, her tone steadier this time. "There's an update about Niyah. You might want to sit down for this."

"So, this guy... Malik Johnson... he was with her that night?"

"Yes," she confirmed. "Marcus took a picture of his SUV, and now the police are looking for him."

"I don't know what to say... I just can't believe it."

"I know, Dad," she said softly. "None of us can."

After hanging up, she sat for a moment in silence.

Detective Samuels leaned back in his chair, staring at the photos on his computer screen. The tan SUV with dark tinted windows filled the frame. He now had both a name and a vehicle. The pieces were beginning to fall into place. With a few swift clicks, he sent the photo to his team and leaned forward to dial the number for the station's media liaison. It was time to make this public.

"Let's get this out to the press," Samuels said the moment the liaison picked up. "We have a name for the man last seen with Niyah on the day of her disappearance. We need to plaster his face and this truck all over the news, on social media, everywhere."

"You got it, Samuels," the liaison responded. "Send me everything you have. We'll make sure it's up within the hour."

Samuels sent over the details and leaned back, his mind running through the next steps. Malik had been a ghost up until now, someone who had stayed under the radar, but with this new information, he couldn't hide for long. Once the photos were out there, people would be looking for him.

He picked up his phone and dialed Marcus. When the young man answered, Samuels wasted no time. "Thank you for your help. I wanted you to know that I forwarded the picture to the media outlets and that it's going to be on the news some time today."

"It's about time."

"You and your family can be assured that the photo of the SUV and Malik's name are going to be all over the news and social media in the next few hours."

"Good," he replied, his voice tense but determined. "If he's out there, someone will spot him."

"You did the right thing by taking that picture. Now, we just need the public's help to track him down."

After hanging up with Marcus, Samuels turned his focus back to the case file. He knew Malik wouldn't stay hidden for long. With his name and vehicle being broadcast to millions, it was only a matter of time before a tip came in. Samuels made sure his team was ready to follow up on any leads.

Chapter 24

By the end of the day, the media blitz was in full effect. News stations were flashing Malik's name and the image of the tan SUV across screens, while social media posts circulated faster than wildfire. Comments and shares piled up, with people across the city pledging to keep an eye out.

Samuels watched the reports roll in, feeling a flicker of hope. He knew Malik wouldn't be able to stay hidden forever. Every minute that passed, the circle was closing tighter around him.

"Malik Johnson, wherever you are," Samuels muttered under his breath, "We're coming for you."

As the hours passed, Detective Samuels monitored the influx of tips. Most were dead ends; people claiming to have seen similar SUVs or men matching Malik's description but each one was tracked and followed. He could feel the tension building from his team from all the calls. But he had faith that sooner or later, the right lead would come through, and this came would be cleared. Every officer in the precinct had been briefed and was ready to mobilize the second they got a solid lead on Malik's location.

Meanwhile, the post was going viral on social media. People were tagging friends, sharing their own theories, and spreading the information faster than the police could keep up with. Some claimed they had seen the tan SUV days ago, while others warned their communities to stay vigilant.

As the public's eyes became an extension of the investigation, Samuels felt the net closing around Malik. It was only a matter of time now. The city was on high alert, and the pressure was mounting. Malik could run, but there was nowhere left for him to hide.

Malik sat in the dim light of his apartment, the TV murmuring in the background. His eyes darted nervously toward the window every few minutes. He hadn't gone out much in the past couple of days. His guilty conscience was feeling the pressure build as the police investigation into Niyah's disappearance intensified. He told himself he had covered his tracks, that no one could tie him to anything. But the anxiety gnawed at him all the same. He flipped through the channels, searching for something to distract him, when the news anchor's voice caught his attention.

"*Breaking news. The police have identified a person of interest in the investigation of Niyah Thompson's death. Malik Johnson, who was last seen with Ms. Thompson the night of her disappearance, is now wanted for questioning. The police are asking anyone with information on his whereabouts or this vehicle to come forward immediately.*" A photo flashed on the screen: his tan SUV with dark-tinted windows, parked outside the same apartment building where he had picked up Niyah. Malik was scared, then pissed. "*Why that bitch! How dare she take a picture of my car,*" He thought to himself. "*It's like she didn't even trust me.*" The camera zoomed in on the vehicle, and then the next image appeared: his face. A mugshot from years ago, but it was unmistakable. The image burned into his mind, and a cold wave of panic washed over him.

The anchor continued, her voice steady and clear. "*Authorities believe Malik Johnson may be connected to the events surrounding Ms. Thompson's disappearance and subsequent death. If you see this man or recognize this vehicle, please contact law enforcement immediately. Do not approach him, as he may be dangerous.*"

Malik stood up so fast he knocked over the beer can on the coffee table. His mind raced. How the hell had they connected him? He had been careful; no witnesses, no real ties. Except for that one thing. That stupid SUV. He cursed under his breath, pacing the room. He knew now that his time was running out. The police weren't just looking for him, they were closing in.

Grabbing his jacket, Malik snatched up his keys. His mind raced as he realized he had to leave, had to disappear before they caught him. They had his face, his name, his vehicle. He couldn't risk staying here another minute. But where would he go? He had to think, and fast. With one last glance at the TV, where his name and face still flashed on the screen, Malik knew his life as he knew it was over.

Malik was frantic as he dialed Tony's number. His mind was still reeling from the news broadcast. He didn't know if Tony had seen it yet, but if they were going to move, they needed to do it fast. The phone rang once, twice, and then Tony's familiar gruff voice answered.

"Yeah?"

"It's me," Malik said, his voice low and strained. "Did you see the news?"

There was a pause on the other end. "Yeah, I saw it," Tony replied, his voice sharp. "They got your face plastered everywhere, man. And that truck? You're done if you don't handle it."

"That's why I'm calling you," Malik muttered, pacing the small apartment. "I need your help again. We gotta get rid of it. Now."

Tony grunted. "This is the last time. Meet me at the old lot off Benson. I'll bring what we need."

Malik hung up without another word, his heart pounding in his chest. He grabbed his jacket, shoved a few things into a bag, and hurried out the door. The streets felt narrower and darker, as if they were closing in on him. His pulse quickened with every step toward the SUV. He glanced around paranoid as he climbed in and started the engine. Driving through the city, Malik kept his eyes peeled for cops or anyone who might recognize him. The news had spread like wildfire, and every second in that truck felt like an eternity.

By the time he pulled into the abandoned lot, Tony was already there. He was leaning against his own car with a gas can in hand. The lot was quiet, surrounded by crumbling buildings and overgrown weeds. It was the perfect place for something to disappear. Malik parked the SUV in the middle of the lot, his hands sweating on the steering wheel.

Tony walked over, his face grim. "We burn it, it's gone. But we gotta do it clean. No traces."

Malik nodded, stepping out of the vehicle. "Let's get it over with."

Without another word, Tony began pouring gasoline over the seats, splashing it on the dashboard, the floor mats, everywhere. The strong smell of fuel filled the air, making Malik's head spin. He stood by the SUV, watching as Tony methodically soaked every inch. It was surreal to think that just days ago, this car had been nothing more than transportation, and now it was a ticking time bomb, evidence that could seal his fate.

When the can was empty, Tony tossed it aside and pulled out a lighter from his pocket. He glanced at Malik one last time.

"You ready for this?" Tony asked, his eyes dark.

Malik hesitated for a second, then nodded. "Do it."

Tony flicked the lighter and tossed it into the SUV. The fire ignited instantly, flames licking up the sides of the vehicle, roaring to life. Malik stepped back, the heat hitting him like a wave. They watched in silence as the fire engulfed the SUV, turning the tan vehicle into a blazing inferno. Smoke billowed into the night sky, and the flames danced wildly, consuming the evidence.

As the fire raged, Malik felt a strange mix of relief and dread. The SUV, the one thing tying him to Niyah's disappearance, was being destroyed. But he knew this wouldn't be the end. The cops were closing in, and no amount of fire could erase what he had done.

"Let's get out of here," Tony said, his voice low as he turned toward his car.

Malik nodded, casting one last glance at the burning wreckage before following Tony. They got into Tony's car and sped off into the night, leaving the inferno behind. Malik stared out the window, knowing that even though the SUV was gone, the truth would catch up with him sooner or later.

As they drove through the streets, Malik's mind churned with thoughts of what had just transpired. The flames had consumed not only the vehicle but also the remnants of his carefully constructed façade. He felt a mix of relief and dread, the adrenaline still coursing through his veins. With the SUV destroyed, he had bought himself a moment of reprieve, but he couldn't shake the feeling that the worst was yet to come.

Tony glanced over, his expression a mix of concern and determination. "You need to lay low for a while, man. You can't keep running like this." Malik nodded, understanding the gravity of his situation. He was in deep, and the longer he stayed exposed, the greater the chance of being discovered. As the city lights blurred past, he began to formulate a plan. One that involved trust on a risky alliance. He knew that the shadows would soon be chasing him, and if he was going to survive, he needed to be one step ahead of them.

Chapter 25

Malik sat on the edge of his bed, the faint light of dawn creeping through the blinds. His nerves were shot after the night he'd had. The image of the SUV burning, flames crackling in the dark, stayed with him, but the relief was short-lived. The city felt smaller, as if every street corner held the eyes of someone who'd seen his face on the news. He needed to leave now. There was no other option.

He rubbed his temples, trying to quell the rising tide of panic. The weight of his choices pressed down on him, a reminder of the tightrope he was walking. He reached for his phone, scrolling through messages in search of a lifeline, someone who could help him slip away undetected. Every name that appeared felt like a potential betrayal; trust was a luxury he could no longer afford.

Malik continued to scrolled through his contacts until he found the number he hadn't dialed in years. His sister Tasha. If anyone could help him, it was her. But he hadn't spoken to his family much in recent years, always keeping his distance, too proud to ask for anything. Now, that distance felt like a wall. But he had no choice. He dialed her number, his heart pounding as it rang.

"Hello?" Tasha's voice came through, cautious, like she already knew what he was calling for.

"Tasha, it's me," Malik said, his voice low. "I need help."

There was a brief silence. "Malik? Do you know what kind of trouble you're in? I saw your face on the news. Mom and Dad saw it too."

"I know," Malik said quickly, panic creeping into his voice. "I didn't want it to be like this, but I need to get out of the city, Tasha. I don't have anywhere else to go."

Tasha's sigh came through the line, heavy with frustration and fear. "Malik, this is serious. They're saying you were the last person with that woman. They're looking for you. What did you do?"

Malik's throat tightened. He couldn't tell her everything, not over the phone. "Look, I just need a place to lay low for a while. You think you can help me out?"

"I don't know, Malik," Tasha said, her voice wavering. "Mom's freaking out, Dad's furious, and everyone's saying you're dangerous. I don't know if we can risk it."

Malik rubbed his forehead, feeling the pressure mounting. "Tasha, please. I'm your brother. I just need to get out of here. If the cops find me, I'm done. I don't have anywhere else to turn."

Another pause, longer this time. Malik could hear her weighing the risks. His desperation hung in the air between them.

"I'll talk to Mom," Tasha finally said. "But don't get your hopes up. This isn't like before. You can't just run, Malik. They're after you for real this time."

"Just... try, okay?" Malik said, his voice barely a whisper. "Let me know what she says."

He hung up, the silence of the room crashing back down on him. Malik knew Tasha had always been the bridge between him and the rest of the family, but the walls felt higher now, harder to cross. He had no idea if his parents would help, and the clock was ticking.

A few minutes later, his phone buzzed. It was a message from Tasha: *Mom says you can come to her place for a night, but after that, you're on your own. We can't do more than that.*

Malik exhaled, a mix of relief and dread tightening in his chest. He had a place to go, but he knew it wouldn't last. One night. He needed to figure out his next move fast.

Malik had just slipped his phone back into his pocket when it buzzed again. His first thought was that it was Tasha calling back with more updates from his mom. But when he glanced at the screen, his stomach twisted. It wasn't Tasha.

It was Camille, his ex-wife. Malik stared at the phone for a moment, his mind racing. He hadn't spoken to Camille in over two years, not since the messy end of their marriage. She had moved on and started a new life without him. He hadn't expected to hear from her ever again. So why now?

With a deep breath, he answered.

"Malik," Camille's voice came through the line, tight with a mixture of shock and anger. "What the hell have you gotten yourself into?"

He closed his eyes, already feeling the weight of the conversation before it even started. "I don't have time for this right now. I know you've seen the news.."

"Damn right I've seen it!" she interrupted, her voice sharp. "Your face is all over every channel! Do you realize what kind of mess you're in? What did you do to that girl?"

"I didn't do anything to her!" Malik snapped, more out of reflex than conviction. His hands clenched into fists. "It's not like that."

"Then what is it like?" Camille pressed. "Because right now, it looks like you're running from the cops, and they're saying you're the last person to see that woman alive."

"You don't know the whole story."

"Then tell me, because right now, I'm just trying to figure out how the man I used to be married to is on the run like a criminal."

There was a long silence. Malik could hear the hurt and disbelief in her voice, but he didn't have the energy to explain everything. Not now.

"I made some mistakes, alright?" he said. "But I didn't hurt her. I just... things got out of control. Now I'm in deep, and I'm trying to fix it."

"If you didn't hurt her then why is your name and face on the news? Why do the police want to talk to you? As usual you mess things up and try to fix it by running away," Camille sounded incredulous. "Malik, you're a fucking idiot and just making it worse."

"I didn't have a choice!" he nearly shouted, the pressure of everything boiling over. "You think I want to be in this mess? I'm doing what I have to do to stay alive!"

Camille paused, and when she spoke again, her voice was quieter. "You know that you need to turn yourself in. This isn't going to end well if you keep running. You have a son, remember? What are you going to do if you get caught? You think this won't come back on him?"

The mention of his son hit Malik like a punch to the gut. He hadn't seen Isaiah in months, hadn't been a part of his life since the divorce. But the thought of his son, knowing that one day he might find out what was happening, gnawed at him.

"I don't know what to do, Camille," Malik admitted, his voice barely a whisper now. "I'm just trying to survive."

"You can't outrun this," Camille said softly. "And you won't be able to look Isaiah in the eyes as long as you're running away. You need to talk to the police."

"That is something that I can't do."

CHAPTER 25   – | 155 |

Another pause stretched between them. Camille sighed, her voice weary. "I guess you don't realize that whatever happened affects her family too. She has children. You need to stop this before it's too late."

Malik didn't answer. He knew she was right, but he couldn't turn himself in. Not yet. Not when he didn't know what the cops had or how much trouble he was really in.

"Just...make the right decision," Camille said after a long silence. "For Isaiah's sake." Then, without waiting for a response, she hung up.

Malik sat there for a long time, staring at the phone in his hand, his heart heavy. Camille's words echoed in his mind, but he shoved them aside. He didn't have time to dwell on what could've been. All he had now was survival. And the clock was ticking.

He sat on the couch thinking how was he going to get to his parents without a truck. He couldn't walk there or Uber since he would easily be noticed. He hated to call his sister again since she had already put her neck out by convincing their parents to let him stay the night. Now, he needed one more favor from her. He just hoped that she wouldn't hang up on him.

The phone rang once, twice, and then Tasha's voice came through, weary and strained.

"What now, Malik?"

"I need one more favor, Tasha," Malik said quickly, not giving her a chance to push back. " I need a ride to our parents."

Tasha sighed, "I told you, Malik, you can't keep dragging us into this. You're putting all of us at risk. You're lucky Mom even let you stay the night after everything."

"I know, I know," he said, rubbing his forehead. "But I'm out of options. I just need to get there, lay low for a few hours, and I'm gone by tomorrow morning. I will make arrangements to get out of the city once I'm there."

Tasha was silent for a moment. He could hear her breathing on the other end, could feel the weight of her hesitance. She had been the only one in the family still willing to talk to him, and even that was fading fast.

"You swear this is the last time?" she asked, her voice sharp. "No more calls, no more asking for rides, no more pulling me into your mess?"

Malik's stomach twisted. He knew that even if he promised, things might get worse before they got better. But right now, all he needed was for her to say yes. "I swear, Tasha. Just get me to Mom and Dad's tonight, and you won't hear from me again."

There was another long pause, then she let out a deep breath. "Fine. I'll pick you up. But after this, Malik, you're on your own. I mean it."

"Thank you," Malik said, relief flooding his voice. "I'll owe you big time."

"You already do," she muttered before hanging up.

Malik slid his phone back into his pocket, feeling the weight of his sister's words. He knew she was right. He had pulled her and his family into a mess they didn't deserve. But right now, survival was the only thing on his mind. He had to keep moving, keep running. He couldn't afford to think about the consequences, not yet.

When Tasha pulled up in her old sedan about thirty minutes later, Malik climbed into the passenger seat without a word. She barely glanced at him, her face tight with anger and exhaustion. They drove in silence, the city lights flashing by as they headed toward their parents' house. The quiet between them was suffocating, but Malik didn't dare speak. He had already asked for too much.

As they neared their parents' neighborhood, Tasha finally broke the silence.

"Malik, I don't know what you're mixed up in, but you need to figure out a way to stop this. Running isn't going to solve anything."

"I know," he muttered, staring out the window. "I'm working on it."

Tasha shot him a skeptical glance. "Are you? Because it doesn't seem like you are."

Malik didn't respond. He didn't have the energy to argue, and deep down, he knew she was right. But admitting it wouldn't change anything.

They pulled up to their parents' house, and Tasha put the car in park.

"Last time," she reminded him, her eyes hard. "After tonight, you're on your own."

"I get it," Malik said, opening the door. "Thanks, Tasha. For everything."

Chapter 26

Malik stepped out of the car and walked up the driveway, his stomach churning. The lights were on, but the house was unusually quiet. His stepfather Michael was the first to appear, emerging from the kitchen with a hard, unyielding expression. His eyes immediately locked onto Malik's, disappointment radiating off him like heat from a furnace.

Malik braced himself as Michael's gaze bore into him, the silence thick with unspoken accusations. The kitchen light cast harsh shadows across the room, amplifying the tension that hung in the air. Malik could feel the weight of his choices pressing down on him, every second stretching into an eternity. He knew this moment was inevitable, a confrontation long overdue, and he prepared for the fallout.

"Malik." Michael's voice was low, a mixture of restrained anger and sadness. "Why the hell are you here?"

Malik couldn't meet his stepfather's gaze, his shoulders slumping under the weight of his guilt. "I messed up Mike," he mumbled, barely able to get the words out. "I didn't mean for it to go this far. I didn't—"

His stepfather cut him off with a sharp wave of his hand. "Didn't mean for it to go this far?" His voice rose, trembling with barely controlled fury. "You think being hunted by the police wasn't going 'too far'? You've got the whole damn city talking about you, Malik.

You've put this family in the middle of your mess, and for what? To save your own skin?"

Malik flinched at the harsh words but said nothing. He didn't have a defense, at least not one that would satisfy his stepfather. Before he could respond, his mother appeared from the laundry room, her eyes wide with worry. She rushed to Malik when she saw her son standing there. "Oh, Malik..." she breathed, her voice filled with a softness that only a mother could muster.

She crossed the room quickly, wrapping her arms around him before he could protest. Malik stood still, caught in her embrace, feeling the warmth and love he hadn't felt in what seemed like years. Her touch was familiar, comforting, but it also stirred the shame deep inside him. His mother had always had a weak spot for him, and he knew it. No matter how much trouble he found himself in, she'd always look at him with that same tenderness. But his stepfather? That was a different story.

His mother stepped back, her hands still gripping his arms as if she were afraid he might disappear. "What have you gotten yourself into, baby?" she asked, her voice trembling with emotion. "You should've come to us sooner. We could've helped you before things got this bad."

Michael snorted, folding his arms over his chest. "Help him? He's beyond help, Sandra. Look at him." He gestured to Malik, his eyes narrowing in disappointment. "He is wanted by the police for questioning, for crying out loud. He's running from the law like a damn criminal."

"He's still our son," his mother shot back, her voice wavering but firm. "He made a mistake, but he's here now. That means something."

"A mistake?" His father's voice rose again, but this time there was a bitterness to it. "He isn't a child in school, Sandra. This is a normal pattern for him. He makes bad decisions and wants us to fix it. Not this time. You have to let him learn on his own. He's already got us involved by coming here. Not to mention our daughter. I will not be an accomplice in this. His ass needs to go tonight or I will call the police and let them know that he's here."

Malik remained silent, absorbing the weight of his stepfather's words. The disappointment in Michael's eyes stung more than anything else. He had always tried to prove himself but standing here now, he realized just how far he had fallen short. And this time, he wasn't sure if there was a way back.

Sandra wasn't ready to give up on him. She cupped his face in her hands, searching his eyes for something , some glimpse of the boy she had raised. "Malik, you've got to turn yourself in. This running... it's only going to make things worse. You can't live like this."

Malik nodded, his throat tight with emotion. "I know, Momma. I'm going to. I just... I needed to see you both first."

Michael let out a long, frustrated sigh. "You should've thought about that before you got in this mess."

"Michael," Sandra said, her voice pleading. "Please, don't be so hard on him. He's here. He's ready to face it now."

Michael's eyes flickered with a mix of anger and pain as he stared at Malik. "I can't feel sorry for him, Sandra. Real men own up to their mistakes. The sooner he can face what happened, whatever it is, the sooner he can face the consequences.."

Malik finally looked up. "I know I fucked up, Mike. I know you're disappointed, and you have every right to be. But I'm not running anymore. I'm turning myself in tomorrow."

Michael studied him for a long moment before speaking. "You'd better. Because if you don't, there's nothing left for us to do for you." He walked out the room before Malik could respond. Malik sat down on the couch and put his head in his hands. Sandra sat next to him. She knew her son would need someone to support him throughout it all. They sat there in silence. Finally she said softly and with concern, "Have you thought about your son? About how this is going to affect him?"

Malik's breath caught in his throat. He had tried to push thoughts of his son Isaiah to the back of his mind through all of this, but hearing his mother mention him brought the guilt crashing down in waves. Isaiah was just six years old, full of life, and completely unaware of the mess his father had made. He hadn't seen his boy in months, but the thought of him growing up without his father there tore him apart.

"I've been thinking about him every day," Malik said, his hands rubbing his face in frustration. "But how can I fix this? Camille's not going to bring him to visit me. She hasn't forgiven me for how things ended between us, and now this? There's no way she'll let him near me when I'm in prison."

Sandra's eyes filled with sympathy, and she leaned closer to him. "Maybe she won't, at least not at first. But Isaiah's going to grow up one day, and he'll want to know who his father is. What matters is that you make the effort to show him you care, even from inside those walls. It's not too late for that."

"I know her. She'll cut me off completely," Malik muttered shaking his head. "I screwed up, and she's not going to let my son anywhere near me after this."

Michael came back in the room standing in the doorway. "You can't control what Camille does but you can control what you do next. If you want a relationship with Isaiah then you're going to have to prove you're worth his time. Even if that takes years. What matters is that you try."

Malik's chest tightened. The thought of losing his son's connection felt like a punishment even worse than prison. He nodded, though doubt still clouded his mind. "I just don't want him to grow up thinking I abandoned him."

"You won't if you keep showing him that you're still his father, no matter what,"Sandra said gently. "But you need to start by doing the right thing tomorrow. This is the first step, Malik. You've got a long road ahead, but at least you're finally taking it."

Chapter 27

The sun had barely risen when the smell of burning rubber and charred metal filled the air over the abandoned lot on the edge of town. A thick column of black smoke spiraled into the sky, drawing the attention of an early morning jogger who lived nearby. As he approached, his heart raced at the sight of the flames licking at the wreckage, the ominous crackling of burning debris punctuating the eerie stillness of the morning. It was a scene straight out of a nightmare, and he quickly dialed the emergency number.

By the time the fire department arrived, the SUV was already reduced to a smoldering shell, the remnants of its once tan exterior now a charred skeleton. Firefighters worked diligently to contain the blaze, but the damage was done. As they sprayed the remains with water, a sense of unease settled over the crowd that had begun to gather, whispers circulating about what had happened. The jogger couldn't shake the feeling that this wasn't just a random fire; it was a marker of something deeper, a signal that trouble was brewing just beneath the surface of their quiet town.

As they continued to douse the flames, one of the firefighters noticed the remains of a license plate barely hanging from the back bumper. It was blackened but still legible. Without hesitation, he called it in. The police arrived within minutes, setting up a perimeter around the scene. The media wasn't far behind cameras rolling, reporters speaking into microphones, feeding the story of the mysterious burning vehicle to the public. It wasn't long before the plates were traced back to Malik Johnson.

Detective Samuels stood just beyond the caution tape, his face a mask of calm as he watched the wreckage being examined. He'd been chasing leads on Malik for days, but this? This felt like the break they needed. The SUV that had been described in the reports, tan with dark tinted windows, was now a heap of twisted metal. But the plates were enough to tie it back to Malik.

Samuels turned away from the scene, pulling out his phone. His mind was racing, not just with the evidence, but with the thought of how Myia would take the news. He had promised to keep her updated, to help her find some closure in the whirlwind of her mother's disappearance.

He dialed Myia's number, and after a few rings, she picked up. "Myia? It's Detective Samuels."

Her voice came through, a little groggy from sleep. "Detective? Is there... is there news?"

Samuels took a breath, choosing his words carefully. "Yes, there's been a development. Early this morning, we received an anonymous call about a vehicle on fire at an abandoned lot. It looks like the SUV matches the description of the one your mother was last seen in, with Malik Johnson."

Myia was silent for a moment, processing the information. "Did you find anything? Inside the car, I mean... anything that would help?"

"The vehicle is completely burned, but we've confirmed that the plates trace back to Malik. It's going to be difficult to find physical evidence inside, but this connects him to the scene. The fire department and our team are going over everything now."

"So he tried to destroy it..." Myia's voice trembled slightly, the weight of what that meant settling in.

"It appears that way," Samuels said gently. "But this puts us one step closer. The fact that he's trying to cover his tracks means he's feeling the pressure. We're also going to release more information to the media and social networks his name, the vehicle, everything we can to put the heat on him."

Myia exhaled sharply, fighting back the emotions that swirled inside her. "Do you think you'll find him soon?"

Samuels' voice was steady, reassuring. "We're closing in. He's on the run, but with this kind of attention, he can't hide forever. We'll find him, Myia. I promise you that."

There was a pause, and then Myia spoke again, quieter this time. "Thank you for keeping me updated. I just... I want this to be over."

Samuels replied. "I understand. I'll call you as soon as we have more. Stay strong." He hung up the phone and looked back toward the smoldering remains of the SUV. Malik was getting desperate, and desperate men made mistakes.

It didn't take long for the news to spread like wildfire. The moment the story broke about the burnt SUV tied to Malik Johnson, social media lit up with speculation, updates, and frenzied commentary. News outlets quickly posted articles with headlines like "Burnt SUV Linked to Fugitive Malik Johnson: Police Closing In" and "Breaking: Malik Johnson's Vehicle Found in Mysterious Fire."

Photos of the charred vehicle, with firefighters standing in the background and police tape flapping in the wind, circulated online. The image was strikingp; a symbol of desperation, a clue in a mystery that had gripped the city. And with it, the public's fascination with Malik deepened.

The media seized on the story, framing it as a gripping narrative of a man on the run, heightening the fascination with Malik and the circumstances surrounding him. News segments dissected every detail, from the SUV's destruction to the lingering questions of his whereabouts. It wasn't just a crime story anymore; it had evolved into a cultural phenomenon, drawing in those who felt both fear and empathy for a figure they hardly knew. With each passing hour, the spotlight intensified, leaving Malik's fate hanging in the balance as the city held its breath, captivated by the unfolding drama.

Twitter threads exploded with theories and opinions, people debating Malik's whereabouts, and what his next move might be. The hashtags #MalikJohnson, #BurntSUV, and #Manhunt started trending within hours. Everyone seemed to have an opinion.

Instagram stories and TikTok videos popped up, with armchair detectives sharing clips of the burned SUV site and discussing the timeline of Malik's disappearance. Some even went as far as driving by the abandoned lot to take their own videos, eager to capture a piece of the action. A video of the news broadcast, with the smoldering SUV in the background, racked up thousands of views within minutes.

The story reached beyond local news, catching the attention of national outlets. Reports highlighted Malik's connection to the missing Niyah,and the SUV that matched the description from the night she vanished. Journalists pieced together timelines, interviews with friends and family, and investigative updates. It was as if the entire city, and the internet, was now looking for him.

Back at Myia's apartment, her phone buzzed relentlessly with notifications. Every social media platform was buzzing with updates about Malik, and it was impossible to escape it. She scrolled through her feed, her stomach turning as she saw post after post about the burnt SUV and his growing infamy. Each headline felt like a knife twisting in her gut, amplifying her anxiety and fear for him.

Her friends and acquaintances were messaging her, sending links, asking if she had heard the latest. She hadn't told anyone about the police updates or about how closely this was tied to her own family's pain. And now, her mother's last moments, including the man she left with, were part of an online frenzy. It felt overwhelming.

Myia sat on the edge of her bed holding her phone tightly. The relentless updates about Malik and the burning SUV filled her with a growing sense of helplessness. She couldn't escape it. No matter where she turned, the news kept coming, and her thoughts drifted to her mother. How this all started and how the world now seemed to know more than she did.

Chapter 28

Miya felt alone and she needed to talk to someone who understood her pain. Without thinking, she dialed her aunt because she didn't want to face this alone. She wanted to hear her calming voice. The phone rang twice before her aunt answered.

"Myia?" Janelle's voice was filled with concern, likely already aware of the latest developments. "I was just about to call you. Have you seen the news? About Malik?"

Myia exhaled, a mix of relief and frustration flooding her chest. "Yeah... Detective Samuels called me earlier about it. I've also seen it on the news. Everyone has. It's all over social media too."

"I can't believe it," Janelle said, her voice tight with emotion. "The fact that he's still out there, and now this burning his car? He's running, and it feels like we're just waiting for the next thing to happen."

"I can't do this, Nelly," Myia admitted, her voice barely above a whisper. "I keep thinking about Mom, and how she's never coming back. And Malik is still out there... running from the cops. I can't stand it."

She was quiet for a moment, letting Myia's words hang in the air. When she spoke again, her voice was calm but firm. "None of us knew who Malik really was, and we couldn't have predicted this. Your mother made her own choices, and so did Malik. This isn't on you."

"I know…" Myia trailed off. She thought of how close she had come to the danger; how her mother had left that night, and how none of them knew it would be the last time they saw her.

"I know it's hard. But you're stronger than you think. And you're not alone in this. We will get through this. All of us, together. We'll make sure Malik faces what he's done, and we'll make sure your mom's memory is honored."

"I just want it to be over," Myia said, her voice breaking. "I can't stand seeing his face everywhere, knowing what he's done. I want him caught. I want him to pay for what he did to Mom."

"And he will. He's running, but he can't hide forever. Detective Samuels and the police will find him, and when they do, he's going to answer for everything."

The words gave Myia a small sense of comfort, but the fear still lingered, heavy in her chest. "Thanks, Auntie. I needed to hear that."

"I'm here anytime, honey," she replied. "Call me whenever you need to talk, okay? "

Myia said. "I will. Thanks."

Myia stood in the kitchen, staring at the phone she had just placed down, feeling like the ground beneath her was shifting. Her aunt's words had offered a temporary sense of comfort, but as the minutes ticked by, the weight of everything that had happened since her mother's disappearance pressed in on her once again. Malik was out there, still free, and the anger she had buried deep inside her was beginning to boil over.

She knew the clock was ticking. Every second that Malik evaded capture was another second of fear or another second of unknown danger. The police were closing in, but the longer he was on the run, the more it felt like the world was holding its breath. And all she could do was wait too, hoping that this nightmare would soon come to an end.

Marcus sat at the kitchen table, scrolling through his phone with a grim expression. The notifications had been constant all morning, each one pushing him closer to the edge. Every update made his blood boil a little more. The rumors, the whispers, and the accusations made it feel like the world was closing in, and there was nothing he could do to stop it.

"You okay?" she asked, her voice small despite the volume of thoughts racing through her mind. He didn't immediately answer. He seemed caught in his own storm. His gaze fixed on the space ahead, as if he was trying to fight his way through a sea of regret and anger. Finally, he looked at Miya, his jaw tight.

"No," he said flatly. "I'm not okay. I keep thinking about that night we were all together. We should've pushed more on meeting him. We should've done something more or got some more information on that guy before she left."

Myia felt a knot form in her throat at the mention of her mother. She hadn't said the words out loud to anyone yet, but every thought about her disappearance felt like a fresh wound, the pain never fading.

"I know it hurts," she whispered. "I miss her too. I wish she never downloaded that damn dating app. But like auntie Nelly keep saying, we can't undo what's been done. We can only move forward."

He let out a long breath, his shoulders slumping. He wasn't so sure he believed that, but he nodded anyway. Tyson, who had been silently watching from across the room, finally spoke. His voice was tight with frustration, "I can't believe this guy's still out there," he muttered, shaking his head. "After everything he did... he thinks he can just burn his car and disappear?"

Marcus looked up, his jaw clenched. "He's desperate. But no matter where he runs, he's not getting away with this." He paused, tossing his phone onto the table with a frustrated sigh. "If I ever run into Malik, it's gonna be a bad day for him."

Tyson glanced at his cousin, his eyes narrowing with a shared anger. "You're not the only one. I've been thinking the same thing. After what he did to my mom..." He said balling his fist. "We're not letting this guy get away with what he did to our family."

Marcus feeling the same rage. "If I get the chance to see him before the cops do..."

Tyson finished his sentence for him. "It'll be over for him. No question." The two cousins sat in silence for a moment, both of them lost in their thoughts. The anger was raw, but beneath it, there was also a sense of helplessness. Malik had hurt their family in a way they could never forget, and the fact that he was still out there, evading capture, made it even harder to swallow.

Just don't do anything reckless, okay?" Myia said, her voice laced with concern. "We need to leave this to the police. If you do something crazy, it's just going to make everything worse."

Tyson's expression hardened. "I know. But if it comes down to it, I won't sit back and let him hurt any more people."

There was a moment of silence as the three of them sat in the heavy quiet of the room, each one processing the anger, fear, and grief in their own way. The sound of a car pulling into the driveway broke the silence, and Myia's heart gave a small jump in her chest. She wondered who it was since she'd already spoken to her aunt earlier. She looked at the camera and saw it was Jordan. She knew he was working a lot, but she didn't know how much he knew about the updates.

She opened the door as soon as he stepped on the porch.

"Hey," he said quietly, looking at her before glancing toward Marcus and Tyson.

"Hey," Myia replied, shutting the door behind him. "We're... hanging in there. Barely."

Jordan walked further into the room, his gaze shifting between them. "I wanted to check on you . I know the past couple of days have been... heavy."

Marcus looked up, his expression hard. "Heavy? That's putting it lightly, bruh."

Jordan sighed and sat down in the armchair across from Tyson. "I know. I get it. But you know how I am ."

"Did you hear the news?" Myia asked, sitting beside Tyson and folding her hands in her lap.

Jordan frowned. "What news?"

Myia hesitated, looking over at Marcus as if silently asking him to explain.

"They found the SUV," Marcus said flatly. "What's left of it, anyway. Malik burned it. He's trying to cover his tracks."

Jordan's expression darkened. "Burned it? Damn... and now he's on the run?"

Tyson nodded. "That's what they're saying. They don't know where he is, and I don't think they're anywhere close to finding him."

Jordan leaned forward, resting his elbows on his knees. "Man... I don't even know what to say. It feels like every time we get news, it just gets worse."

"It does," Myia whispered. Her voice trembled, but she kept herself composed. "And now, who knows how long it'll be before they find him? If they even do."

"They will," Jordan said firmly. "They have to. There's too many people on this; cops, the media, the whole damn city. Malik can't run forever."

Tyson scoffed, shaking his head. "You think he's stupid? He's already covered his tracks this far. He's a step ahead of everyone."

Jordan said. "Not for long. If the police don't find him, then we're going to take matters into our own hands."

"I'm glad you agree because that's the same thing I said earlier," Marcus said. "He's going to be sorry he ever came across this family."

Chapter 29

After the talk with his parents, Malik knew his time was limited and he didn't want to push it. He needed to get a nap but first he had to make a plan. Tasha had been true to her word; he had one night to lay low, and then he was on his own. Tomorrow morning, he needed to be gone out of his parents house before the cops closed in.

He had to get a ride. But with his face all over the news and the possibility of his SUV being found, he knew his options were limited. He scrolled through his phone trying to see which of his friends would help him. The first person he called was an old friend from high school, Terrence. They hadn't spoken in years, but Malik figured he might be able to help. The phone rang a few times before Terrence picked up.

"Malik?" Terrence's voice was cautious, as if he already knew why he was calling. "What's going on, man?"

"I need a favor," Malik said, trying to sound calm. "I need a ride. I'm getting out of the city for a while."

Terrence was silent for a moment. "I saw the news, man. You know the cops are looking for you, right?"

"I know," Malik replied through gritted teeth. "That's why I need to leave."

"I can't get involved in this, Malik," Terrence said, his voice firm. "You're in too deep. I'm sorry, but I've got a family now. I can't risk it." Before Malik could argue, the line went dead. He let out a frustrated breath. One down.

He scrolled again, this time landing on Devon, a guy he used to work with at a warehouse. Devon had always been down for a hustle, no questions asked. Malik hit the call button and waited. "What's up, Malik?" Devon answered, sounding casual.

"Devon, I need a ride out of town. You think you can help me out?" There was a pause. "You serious? After all that stuff they're saying on the news? No way, man. The cops are looking for you. I'm on probation. I can't get involved in that mess, let alone be talking to you."

Malik's frustration grew. He couldn't catch a break. "You owe me, Devon. Remember when I covered for you at work?"

"Yeah, and I paid that back," Devon said quickly. "This? This is something else, man. You're hot right now, and I'm not about to get burned. Good luck, though." Click.

Malik cursed under his breath. He dialed another number, this time reaching out to an old associate, Malcolm Green. Malcolm was the type to handle shady deals, and Malik figured if anyone could help him, it'd be him.

"Malik, long time," Malcolm answered, his voice smooth. "What's this about?"

"I need a ride out of town," Malik said, cutting to the chase. "And I'm willing to pay." Malcolm let out a low chuckle. "Man, I don't know if you've been watching the news, but you're everywhere right now. I'd love to help, but I'm not trying to be on the police's radar. You're toxic right now. Good luck, though." For a third time, the call ended, leaving Malik stranded and furious. No one wanted to touch him, and with every passing minute, his options were slipping away.

He had one last call to make. His heart pounded as he dialed Lonnie's number. Lonnie wasn't exactly trustworthy, but he knew how to move in the shadows, the kind of guy who could make things disappear. If anyone would help him, it'd be Lonnie, for a price. "Malik," Lonnie answered after the second ring. "I was wondering when you'd call. Saw your face on the news."

"I need a ride out of town," Malik said, getting straight to the point. "You help me, I'll pay whatever you want." Lonnie was silent for a beat, weighing the risk. "I can get you a cash car, no questions asked. But it's gonna cost you. I'm talking real money. You up for that?"

"Yeah, I can handle it," Malik replied, relief flooding his voice. "I've got enough cash to make it worth your while."

"Alright," Lonnie said. "Meet me tomorrow morning at the old scrapyard on the west side. I'll have your car ready. But don't think I'm doing this out of the goodness of my heart. You're paying me big for this, Malik."

"Deal," Malik said without hesitation. He couldn't afford to negotiate. When he hung up the phone, Malik slumped back against the bed. He was feeling the weight of everything pressing down on him. The deal was set, but he had to act fast. He knew Lonnie was only in it for the money, and if anything went sideways, Malik would be on his own again.

He barely slept that night in his old room. This was the place where he decided on his life plans and vowed never to come back again. He'd spent years confined to this room as punishment for whatever reckless act he did as a teenager. Just for him to be back as an adult because of another impulsive decision was his karma for not listening to his parents. He could almost hear their disappointed voices echoing through the walls, reminding him that some mistakes never truly leave you, no matter how far you run.

The next morning, Malik slipped out of his parents' house before dawn, the streets still dark and quiet. He had taken out enough money from his bank account to get a head start, knowing it was risky, but necessary. He couldn't risk staying in the city any longer. As soon as the sun started to rise, every minute would feel like a countdown. With each step, he felt the weight of his decision settle in, but there was no turning back now. He had already crossed a line.

Arriving at the scrapyard, Malik spotted Lonnie standing by an old sedan, a 2007 beige Toyota Camry. It was perfect for flying under the radar. The car blended seamlessly into the landscape of rusted metal and forgotten vehicles, its unassuming exterior offering the anonymity Malik desperately needed. He approached Lonnie, who was casually leaning against the car with a knowing smirk on his face.

"Here she is," he said, tossing Malik the keys. "It ain't pretty, but it'll get you out of town without raising any eyebrows." Malik handed over the cash, more than he could comfortably spare, but it didn't matter. All that mattered was getting out.

"You sure this is gonna work?" Malik asked, his voice tight. Lonnie smirked. "It'll work. Just drive smart and keep your head down. Good luck, Malik. You're gonna need it."

It was something about the way he said it that gave him a bad feeling. "Thanks man. If anyone asks, you haven't seen or spoken to me."

"Why would I snitch on the guy who just paid me. You know I mind my own business. Do you got a plan on where your heading?"

"I'll keep that to myself for now. You can never know who's listening" Malik said as he opened the door. as he slid into the driver's seat, he was caught by the familiar scent of worn fabric and stale air. He knew this wasn't just a car; it was his ticket to slipping away. It was also his chance to find a new path where he could reclaim his freedom. He turned the key in the ignition and the engine rumbled to life as the reality of his next move settled in. Malik pulled out of the lot and started driving. He wasn't sure where he was headed, but he knew one thing for certain: there was no turning back now. The weight of the past few days clung to him like a shadow, urging him to keep moving, to escape the tightening grip of his reality.

The road stretched out before him, a seemingly endless ribbon of cracked asphalt lined with trees that swayed gently in the morning breeze. Every mile he put between himself and Crest Ridge felt like a victory, but the gnawing unease in his chest refused to let him celebrate. He turned on the radio, hoping to drown out his thoughts, but every station seemed to carry a reminder of what he was running from. The blaring sirens of a breaking news segment jolted him, and he quickly switched it off, opting instead for the oppressive silence that mirrored his mood.

As the sun rose, it created a beautiful scenery across the landscape. Malik wanted to stop and take a picture. He glanced at his phone on the passenger seat, tempted to pick it up. But he knew if he did, he would check the news too. And if he did that, then he would see something that he wasn't prepared for. But he resisted, knowing that any slip up or any moment of distraction, could cost him his freedom. Instead, he focused on the road ahead, his mind calculating the next steps. He needed gas, food, and most importantly, a plan. The Camry might have been his escape, but it wouldn't carry him forever. He knew that the walls were closing in, and he could feel the weight of it with every passing second.

Chapter 30

The living room was quiet except for the soft rustling of papers and the occasional sniffle. Janelle sat on the couch, her phone in hand, staring at the screen. She had just posted the announcement on social media, *"A Memorial for Niyah"*, that was scheduled for the following Saturday at Hidden Oaks. The same park where families have celebrated with reunions and picnics over the years would now be known as a place for mourning.

She hadn't realized how heavy it would feel to put her sister's name beside the word *memorial*. It felt surreal, like something out of a bad dream she couldn't wake up from. Janelle's fingers trembled as she scrolled through the comments that had already started appearing below her post. Messages of condolences, heart emojis, and promises of thoughts and prayers brought a sad realization and a fresh reminder of her sister's absence.

She leaned back exhausted as the reality of it all settled in. The police still hadn't released her sister's body yet due to the ongoing investigation. It was a gut-wrenching reminder that this nightmare wasn't over. The family couldn't even bury her and it's been almost two weeks now. But they needed closure. They needed a way to grieve together, to honor Niyah's life, even though it felt incomplete without her physically there.

Zara had suggested the memorial saying they couldn't wait any longer. "We need this, auntie. We can't let her memory be lost in all this mess. First it was my mom and now it's her," she had said, her voice trembling. Janelle had agreed, even though it broke her heart.

Marcus, sitting across the room, scrolled through his phone, occasionally glancing at his mom's post. "Looks like people are already sharing it mom," he said, his voice low. "The whole family's going to be there, and it looks like some of her friends too. It's going to be packed," he said.

She nodded, her throat tight. "Everywhere she went she made a lot of friends. She touched a lot of lives."

Jordan leaning against the wall, crossed his arms. "It's going to be hard going to that park," he said quietly. "She's normally the one who plans all the families activities."

Marcus sighed, "Yeah. It won't feel the same."

Janelle set her phone down and wiped at her eyes. "This is all we can do for now. We can only do so much without a body and remember how much she loved to barbecue for us. Now we'll do it in her memory." She hesitated before adding, "And if anyone hears about Malik... we need to be ready."

Marcus clenched his jaw. "If Malik shows up at that park, it's going to be a bad day for him, mom."

Jordan nodded in agreement "He better not come anywhere near this family again."

Her face changed at the sound of his name. The man responsible for all this pain. "I doubt he will, but we need to focus on Niyah. This day is for her, not him."

As she refreshed her post, she noticed new messages from people offering to help in any way they could. Some volunteered to cater the memorial, while others offered to bring drinks and help set up. It meant so much to the family. In the midst of their grief, these small gestures felt like lifelines, a reminder that they weren't alone in this tragedy. The community was stepping up to ensure that Niyah's memory was honored in the way she deserved.

She wiped away another tear as she read the messages aloud. "People really loved her," she whispered.

"Yeah," Marcus replied, his voice thick with emotion. "She was one of a kind."

Marcus's phone buzzed, interrupting the quiet conversation. The screen lighting up with a notification from an unknown number. He glanced at it with a mix of curiosity and wariness.

"I got info on Malik that you'd really want to know. Message back if you're interested."

His expression hardened, but he quickly tried to mask it, not wanting to worry his mom. Jordan, who was sitting close enough to catch the shift in Marcus's demeanor, gave him a questioning look. "You good?" he asked, his tone low.

Marcus nodded slightly, keeping his voice steady for their mom's sake. "Yeah, just... something came up. I'll check on it later."

But Janelle had already noticed the brief exchange, her motherly instincts kicking in. "Is something wrong?" she asked, her brow creased with concern.

Marcus forced a reassuring smile, pocketing his phone. "It's fine, Mom. Nothing for you to worry about." He glanced at his brother, giving him a look that promised they'd discuss it later.

Janelle went back to reading through the flood of messages. As much as she was focused on organizing the memorial, her thoughts kept drifting to Myia and Tyson. They had both been hit especially hard by their mom's death, and she felt a deep responsibility to do something special for them. Niyah had been their mother, their anchor, and she wanted to make sure they felt supported in a meaningful way during the memorial. No words or actions could fully heal the pain they were feeling. But she could still try to ease it, even just a little.

"I've been thinking," she said softly, breaking the silence. "We should plan something special for Myia and Tyson during the memorial. Something that's just for them, to remind them how much their mom loved them."

Marcus raised his eyebrows. "Like what?"

Janelle paused, tapping her fingers on her knee as she considered. "We could have a private moment for them before everyone else arrives. Just a few minutes for the two of them at the park. They can say their goodbyes in their own way, without a crowd around."

Jordan responded, "That sounds like a great idea mom. It's been so hard with all the attention. Something quiet sounds like it would be just what they need."

She smiled sadly. "I think it's what she would've wanted for them." She began jotting down notes for the memorial, making sure to carve out that private time for Myia and Tyson, knowing that small gesture could mean the world to them.

Marcus leaned forward, resting his elbows on his knees. "Yeah, I think that's a good idea. Tyson's been putting on a brave face, but I can tell it's eating him up inside. And Myia..." He trailed off, shaking his head. "She's been trying to hold everything together, but she's hurting just as much. They both need this."

Janelle nodded, her gaze distant. "They've lost so much, and this memorial... it's for all of us, but especially for them. I want them to feel their mom's presence, to know that she's still with them in some way." Her voice cracked slightly, and she took a steadying breath before continuing. "We can have something symbolic too, like releasing balloons or lighting candles. They need something they can hold onto, something meaningful."

Jordan crossed his arms, nodding thoughtfully. "Balloons might be nice. It's simple, but it's a way for them to send a message to her, you know? Like they're still connected." He glanced at Marcus, who gave a small nod of approval.

Janelle's expression softened. "Then that's what we'll do. We'll make it a moment for them—a moment to remember, to feel close to her again."

Chapter 31

Marcus leaned back in the chair, trying to keep his expression neutral, as he read the message again. His mind raced with who was the sender and how did they get his number. Jordan noticed the shift in his demeanor immediately.

"What's up bruh?" He asked, his curiosity piqued.

Marcus handed him the phone, keeping his voice low so their mom wouldn't hear. "Look at this shit. I don't know if it's real or just someone playing games."

He frowned as he read the message. "They playing with wrong family unless you think it's real."

"I don't know," Marcus replied glancing over at his mom who was still deeply focused on the memorial planning. "But I'm not telling Mom. Not yet."

"Yeah, she's already dealing with enough. But you gotta be careful, man. Whoever sent this could be dangerous or just fucking with you."

He sighed. "I know, but I can't just ignore it. What if they really know something? Malik's still out there."

"If we ever run into that guy, it's gonna be a bad day for him. He put us all through hell."

Marcus agreed. "Let's just keep this between us for now. I'll figure out what to do next." He sat there for a few moments, weighing his options. He typed out a quick response:

How do I know this is real?

He hit send and leaned back, watching his phone intently. Jordan stayed quiet but kept an eye on his brother, clearly feeling the same nervous anticipation. They both waited, the seconds dragging out as tension filled the room. Finally, a new message popped up on the screen.

Because Malik's not in town anymore. You and your family are looking in the wrong places.

His eyes widened as he read the response, his heart pounding. He handed the phone to Jordan, who read the message and glanced back at his brother with a serious look.

"This guy knows something," Jordan said quietly.

"Yeah, but that doesn't mean we can trust him."

Marcus stared at the message, a million thoughts racing through his mind. If Malik was really gone, this could change everything, but they still didn't know who was feeding them this information. He quickly typed out a message, his fingers moving fast as his nerves kicked in. He knew he had to get to the bottom of this, but he wasn't about to be played.

"Meet me at the memorial this Saturday. If what you have is real, show up. And it better not be a waste of my time."

He hit send and sat back, staring at the screen. Jordan leaned closer, watching his brother's every move. "You sure that's a good idea?" he asked, his voice low.

"I don't know," Marcus admitted. "But if this person knows something about Malik, I'm not letting them hide behind a screen. We'll be surrounded by people, and I'll make sure it's safe."

Jordan nodded slowly, but the tension in the room was thick. The idea of some mysterious stranger showing up at the memorial made both of them uneasy, especially with everything that was already going on. But Marcus couldn't shake the feeling that this was his best chance to get closer to the truth. Now, all they had to do was wait and see if this person would show up at Hidden Oaks.

Janelle looked up from her planning, noticing the hushed conversation between the two. They were huddled together, speaking in low voices and glancing at Marcus's phone every few seconds. She narrowed her eyes, suspicion creeping in. "What are you two whispering about over there?" she asked, raising an eyebrow. "Something I need to know?"

They exchanged quick glances, both trying to keep their faces neutral. Marcus was the first to speak, his tone casual, though he could feel his pulse quicken. "Nothing, Mom. Just, you know... talking about the memorial. Seeing if we can help out."

She crossed her arms, clearly not convinced. "You sure about that? Because you both look like you're hiding something."

Jordan quickly chimed in, "Nah, Mom, we're good. Just trying to make sure everything goes smoothly on Saturday."

She sighed, her gaze lingering on them for a moment longer. She knew her boys well enough to tell when something was off, but she was too overwhelmed to press the issue right now. Between organizing the memorial, being the emotional support for all the family and friends, and managing her own grief, her plate was full.

"Alright, but if there's something going on, I better hear about it. We've got enough to deal with as it is."

They nodded quickly, relieved that their mom wasn't pushing further. As she turned her attention back to her notes, the brothers exchanged a silent look. They knew they were walking a fine line, and while they didn't want to keep secrets from their mom, this situation with Malik felt too dangerous to bring her into. At least, not yet.

Marcus, feeling the weight of the lie, stood up abruptly. "I'm gonna step out for a bit," he said, avoiding eye contact with his mom, "I gotta make a call." Jordan gave him a quick nod, understanding what he was about to do.

Out in the hallway, he pulled out his phone and scrolled to Myia's contact. His heart pounded as he dialed her number. After a couple of rings, she picked up.

"Hey," Myia's voice was quiet on the other end. "What's up?"

Marcus glanced back at the closed door behind him, making sure he was alone. "I need to tell you something, but you can't say anything to Mom, alright?"

There was a brief pause before Myia replied, "OK promise. Now what's going on?"

He took a deep breath. "I got a message from some unknown number. They're claiming they know something about Malik, and that he's not in town anymore. I told them to meet me at the memorial this weekend if they're for real."

"Wait, what?" Myia sounded shocked. "And you didn't tell your mom?"

"No," he said firmly. "She's dealing with too much already, and I don't even know if this is legit. I don't want to get her worried over nothing."

Myia hesitated, her voice softer now. "This could be dangerous. What if this person is just messing with you?"

"Jordan knows about it and we've thought about that," he admitted, "but if they know something, I can't just ignore it. We need to know where Malik is."

Myia was silent for a few moments before responding, "Alright. I won't tell your mom. But be careful, okay?"

"Promise," he replied. "I'll keep you updated."

As they ended the call, Marcus stood in the hallway for a moment, his mind racing. He had no idea what would happen at the memorial, but he knew one thing for sure: they were getting closer to finding Malik, one way or another.

Marcus slid his phone back into his pocket and leaned against the wall, his thoughts swirling. He had been cautious about sharing too much with Myia, not wanting to worry her more than necessary. Still, her concern lingered in his mind. She wasn't wrong; this could be dangerous. But the possibility of getting closer to Malik outweighed his hesitation. He couldn't let fear stop him now, not when they were so close.

Taking a deep breath, Marcus pushed himself off the wall and headed into the living room where Jordan was waiting. "She's worried," he said as he sat down.

Jordan glanced up from his phone. "Of course, she is. Everyone is. But if this lead is legit, we have to see it through."

"Yeah, but we can't go into this blindly. We need to be smart about it. Malik's already proven he's desperate."

"Desperate people make mistakes. If he's still out there, we'll catch him slipping sooner or later."

Marcus's expression changed. Deep down he wanted to believe that. But the way it's playing out with no one able to find Malik, he had no choice but to keep pushing forward, no matter the risks.

Chapter 32

Malik sat on the edge of the motel bed, staring at the cracked ceiling as the faint hum of the air conditioner filled the room. He had made it to the next state over, but the temporary relief he felt from getting out of town was already starting to fade. His eyes flicked to the clock on the nightstand. It was well past midnight, but sleep wasn't an option. Not when everything was closing in on him.

Thoughts raced through his mind like a chaotic storm, each one a reminder of the precarious position he was in. He couldn't shake the image of the charred SUV, the remnants of his life back home, and the way the world was now framing him. With the police searching for him and social media buzzing with speculation, he felt like a ghost, haunting the edges of his own existence.

His phone buzzed beside him, a low chime of notifications he had ignored for hours. Reluctantly, Malik picked it up and swiped through the news articles that flashed on his screen. His stomach twisted when he saw the headlines.

"Burnt SUV Linked to Malik Johnson, Suspected in Recent Homicide."

His heart dropped as he scrolled through the details. The police had found the remains of the SUV, torched and abandoned. The plates were traced back to him. Malik's name, once hidden in the shadows, was now front and center in every news update. The media had caught wind of it, and the story was spreading like wildfire.

His hand tightened around the phone. Everything was crumbling faster than he could keep up. He had thought burning the SUV would buy him time, might even throw the cops off his trail for a while. But now, the evidence was staring him right in the face. The police knew which meant everyone else knew. And if they had found the SUV, it wouldn't be long before they found him.

Panic surged in his chest, and Malik stood up, pacing the length of the small motel room. The low light from the bedside lamp flickered, casting his shadow against the wall. His mind raced with thoughts like what was his next move? He couldn't keep using his current phone. He knew that they'd trace it easily. He needed to disappear for real this time, and that meant severing every tie, at least for now.

He stopped pacing, his eyes settling on his phone again. He had to call his parents, let them know he was okay. Well, as okay as he could be given the circumstances. His mother would be worried sick, and his stepfather... well, Malik didn't even want to think about what he was feeling right now.

But calling them from this phone was a risk. The cops could track the number in seconds, and he couldn't afford to make that mistake again. He quickly grabbed his jacket and stuffed his wallet into his pocket. If he was going to make the call, he needed a new phone, something untraceable. A prepaid burner phone would do the trick. It wouldn't last long, but it would give him enough time to make the call without alerting anyone.

Malik left the motel room, moving quickly through the dimly lit parking lot. The streets were quiet and deserted at this hour, but his paranoia kept him glancing over his shoulder every few minutes. The fluorescent lights from the truck stop across the street flickered up ahead and he made a beeline for it, pulling his hood up to stay as inconspicuous as possible.

Inside, the cashier barely looked up from her phone as Malik entered. He walked straight to the electronics section scanning the rows of cheap, prepaid phones. He grabbed the cheapest one along with a small pack of minutes and hurried to the counter.

As the cashier rang up the items, Malik felt his anxiety spike again. His eyes darted to the door, half expecting to see flashing blue lights outside or an officer storming in to arrest him on the spot. But the store was quiet, and the cashier simply handed him the bag with a bored expression.

"Have a good night," she mumbled, returning to her phone without a second glance.

Malik stuffed the phone into his jacket and left the store as quickly as he had come, his nerves still on edge. Once he was back in the motel room he ripped open the packaging and activated the phone. It felt strange using this cheap device after relying on his old one for so long, but it was a necessary precaution.

He dialed his mother's number, holding his breath as he pressed the call button. It rang several times before her familiar voice answered, thick with worry.

"Hello, who is this?"

"Mom, it's me," he said, keeping his voice low. "I'm okay. I'm out of town now."

"Oh, thank God," she breathed, her voice shaky with relief. "We've been worried sick. Michael's been pacing all night. Malik, what are you going to do? The police... they found the SUV."

"I know," Malik muttered, his throat tightening. "I saw it on the news."

"Then you know they're going to get a search warrant for your place. They're closing in on you. This isn't the way, Malik. You have to turn yourself in."

He swallowed hard, guilt and fear gnawing at him. "I can't, Mom. Not yet. I just need some more time to figure things out."

His mother's voice broke. "Malik, please. Running is only going to make this worse."

"I'm not running," he lied, knowing full well that's exactly what he was doing. "I'll call again soon, okay? Just... don't worry about me."

"I'm your mother. Of course I'm going to worry," she whispered, and for a moment, Malik almost regretted calling.

But before he could say more, his stepfather's voice cut through the phone. "Malik, listen to me."

Malik's grip tightened on the phone. "Michael—"

"You need to turn yourself in. Enough of this running around. Do you hear me? They're going to catch you, and when they do, it'll be ten times worse."

"I know," Malik replied, his voice strained. "I just... I can't do that right now. I gotta think and I can't do it there."

There was a heavy pause on the line before Michael spoke again, his tone grim. "You can't outrun this forever, Malik. Sooner or later, it's going to catch up with you."

"I know Mike, I know. It's just that i need ..."

"What you need to do is take responsibility for your actions. You're a grown man with a son. What will that teach him about accountability? A real man would accept the consequences. Your family is to support you, not cover up for your crimes. As a matter of fact, don't think about coming home because I won't allow it."

He hung up before Malik could respond. He sat on the edge of the bed again, staring at the prepaid phone in his hand. He knew his stepfather was right. The clock was ticking, and his time was running out.

Malik slumped back onto the bed, staring up at the ceiling once more. His mind was a tangled mess of fear, regret, and desperation. Every possible plan he considered fell apart the moment he thought about Isaiah. The boy had been the one good thing in Malik's life, the reason he had wanted to be better. But that was before everything spiraled out of control.

Now, Isaiah was at the forefront of every thought. How could he ever explain this to his son? How could he even look him in the eye after what he'd done? The image of him laughing and carefree haunted Malik. He pictured his son growing up without a father, asking his mom where he was, and hearing nothing but bitter words about his mistakes. It tore at him.

He had screwed up in so many ways and now it felt impossible to fix. But he figured that there was still a way out. Something gnawed at the back of his mind. It was a tiny flicker of hope that if he just talked to the police, told them it was an accident, things wouldn't be as bad as they seemed. It's a slim chance that they'd believe that he didn't mean for any of this to happen.

Chapter 33

M alik rubbed his hands over his face, trying to calm the wave of panic that was building. He'd gone too far to turn back now, but the thought of spending the rest of his life behind bars, without any chance of being there for Isaiah made him want to scream. The police could be lenient if he came clean, if he could explain that none of this had been part of the plan.

"It was an accident," Malik muttered to himself. "It wasn't supposed to happen like this."

He stood up pacing again trying to imagine what he would say. He'd tell Detective Samuels that he didn't know things would go so wrong. If he could convince them that it wasn't intentional, that it was all a misunderstanding, then there could be some kind of deal they could work out. He wasn't a cold-blooded killer. He didn't want anyone to die. But he couldn't deny what had happened, and that truth was crushing.

Isaiah's face flashed in his mind again. His wide, curious eyes looking up at him. The thought of his son growing up hearing his name as a criminal was unbearable. Malik knew that Camille would never let him forget it. She'd keep Isaiah away, make sure he knew the kind of man his father was. "I can't let that happen," he whispered.

He thought if he confessed, the truth could set things straight and there would be some mercy in the system. He could admit to burning the SUV, to running because he was scared, but deny any intent to hurt anyone. The fear was real, but so was the hope that he could still salvage something, no matter how small.

But even as Malik clung to that thought, he couldn't shake the sinking feeling that the moment he walked into that police station, the game would be over. They wouldn't care about his reasons or his excuses. They'd see him as nothing more than a criminal; a fugitive who had tried to cover his tracks and failed. And what if they didn't believe him? What if this was the end, and there was no way out after all?

Malik's heart raced again, and he sank onto the bed feeling the weight of his choices crushing him. He wanted to believe there was still hope, but deep down he knew he was running out of time. He had been holed up in the dingy motel for a week, watching the world move on without him. Every day had felt like it stretched on forever, but the ticking of time was louder in his mind than it had ever been. He'd spent countless hours scrolling through his phone, checking the news, waiting for the police to track him down. They hadn't yet but he knew it was only a matter of time.

Every plan he thought up ended the same way: turning himself in. He had burned through most of the cash he had withdrawn, surviving on fast food and the occasional vending machine snack. His life had come down to sitting in a run-down room with the walls closing in, feeling more and more like a ghost of the man he used to be.

The decision had gnawed at him for days. Turning himself in felt like the only option, but he needed something before he could go through with it. He needed to see his parents one last time.

He wanted to talk to his mother, to feel her warmth again, to hear her tell him that everything would be okay, even though he knew that wasn't true. His stepfather would be a different story. But despite everything, Malik needed to see him too. The disappointment in his father's eyes had hurt more than any of Malik's past mistakes. But before he could face the police, before he faced his uncertain future, he needed to go back home. He needed to feel something familiar.

Malik sat up on the bed, rubbing his tired eyes. His phone was in his hand again, and this time, he didn't hesitate to dial his mother's number. It rang twice before she answered.

"Malik?" Her voice sounded as if she had been waiting for him to call.

"Hey, Mom," he said, trying to keep his tone casual. "I know it's early... I just wanted to check in."

There was a pause on the other end, and he could almost see her frowning in that way she did whenever she sensed something was off. "Is everything alright?" she asked slowly. "You sound... different."

"Yeah, yeah, I'm fine," he replied quickly, glancing at the drawn curtains. "I, uh, just wanted to say I'll be by in the morning. Got a few things to handle first."

Another pause. "Malik, what's going on? You know you can tell me anything."

He took a shaky breath, wishing he could be honest with her. But he knew it would only bring more trouble, and he wasn't ready to drag her into it. Not yet. "I'm coming home. I need to talk to you and Mike before I... before I go to the police."

There was a long pause on the other end of the line, and when she finally spoke, her voice cracked with emotion. "Oh, Malik. Are you sure? You know Michael..."

"I know, Mom," he interrupted softly. "I just need to see you both. One more time."

"We'll be here," she said quietly. "Just... please, don't run again."

"I won't," Malik promised, and for the first time in days, he meant it.

After a moment, she sighed. " I love you."

"Love you too, Mom." He ended the call, staring at his phone for a long moment. Then, without another word, he tossed it onto the bed and sat there in silence, feeling more alone than ever.

Malik leaned forward, resting his elbows on his knees as the weight of his decision pressed down on him. His mother's voice lingered in his ears, filled with hope and fear, a stark reminder of the bridges he'd burned and the lives he'd affected. He had spent so long running from his mistakes, from justice, from himself. But now, the thought of facing his family again brought a flicker of something he hadn't felt in a long time: acceptance.

He ran a hand over his face, his resolve faltering. What would Mike say when he showed up? Malik exhaled sharply, his jaw tightening as he thought about Mike. His stepfather had never sugarcoated anything, especially when it came to Malik. They'd had their share of clashes, but deep down, Malik knew Mike had always wanted what was best for him.

Still, he couldn't help but feel a twinge of dread at the thought of facing him now. Mike wouldn't hold back, not after everything Malik had done. But maybe that was what he needed; someone to tell him the truth, no matter how hard it was to hear. Malik rubbed his temples and wondered what Mike would say. Probably why was he here bringing more chaos to their door. But he couldn't avoid it anymore. He needed to face the consequences, even if it meant losing what little connection he still had with his family. The thought was unbearable, but he knew the alternative was worse.

Chapter 34

It was a bright Saturday morning at Hidden Oaks, and the atmosphere was filled with both sorrow and a sense of community. Dozens of people had gathered to honor Niyah's memory, and the grassy area was dotted with chairs, flowers, and photos of her smiling face. Purple and white balloons swayed gently in the breeze tied to various tables and fences. The colors had been chosen by Myia, who knew purple had always been her mom's favorite color. The balloon release was meant to be a symbolic farewell, a small way to release the pain of her absence.

Janelle moved through the crowd, coordinating with the volunteers who had offered to help set up. Several friends and neighbors had brought food and drinks. The tables were filled with trays of catered dishes, homemade casseroles, and jugs of iced tea. Everyone was doing their best to lend a hand. Their shared grief blending into a quiet determination to make the memorial beautiful.

Marcus and Jordan helped carry chairs and set up the sound system for the service. Myia, standing off to the side, looked at the balloons with a distant expression. Her heart was heavy, but the gesture felt right. It was like a small piece of closure in an ocean of unresolved emotions.

The media had already shown up. The cameras were already rolling as reporters stood nearby, trying to capture the mood. The family had expected their presence, given the ongoing investigation and Malik still being a wanted man. But Janelle had done her best to keep the focus on her sister's memory.

Marcus scanned the crowd of both familiar and unfamiliar faces. His mind drifted back to the message he had received earlier in the week. He was on edge, wondering if the mysterious person who claimed to know something about Malik would show up. He felt his phone buzzed, but he ignored it for now. There were too many eyes here, too many people watching. He couldn't make a scene.

Jordan walked over holding a handful of the purple balloons and handed one to Myia. "You alright?" he asked softly. She nodded, but her eyes were clouded with sadness. "It just doesn't feel real. Even with all these people here, it feels like we're just going through the motions."

Jordan looked down, feeling the same way. "I know. But today is all about her. And for us, too. Don't forget that." Marcus overheard their conversation but remained quiet, keeping an eye on the crowd. He glanced at his watch. Whoever sent him that message knew to meet him here today, but he didn't know what to expect. His heart thudded in his chest as the time for the memorial drew closer, and the feeling of anticipation blended with the grief that hung heavy in the air.

The soft hum of conversations grew quieter as more people arrived settling into their places. Myia took a deep breath and looked up at the balloons. She was preparing herself for the moment they would be released, sending their love to the sky in honor of Niyah.

Tyson stood nearby with Ellis and helped him straighten out his shirt. Ellis was visibly anxious. He wasn't used to being around so many people. Darren walked up and placed a comforting hand on Ellis's shoulder.

"You're doing great, big guy," Darren said softly, giving his son a small smile. Ellis nodded but didn't say anything, still processing the gravity of the day. Tyson adjusted his tie and looked out at the crowd. His usually relaxed demeanor was replaced with a quiet seriousness. It was as though the weight of grief settled heavily on his shoulders. It was hard to believe that his mom was gone.

Darren walked over to Janelle who was busy organizing the final touches. He leaned in and asked if she needed anything, making sure everything was on track. She briefly glanced at her sons but quickly looked away. Her heart was heavy with the weight of what she couldn't control. The entire family was struggling to hold it together. But this memorial felt like one step forward, even in the midst of so much pain.

As the time for the balloon release drew closer, everyone began to gather near the center of the park where a small stage had been set up for people to speak. The media was positioned off to the side, cameras pointed at the family, waiting for the moment.

As Janelle gathered her composure, she looked out over the crowd, her heart swelling with pride for the support surrounding her family. "Myia, Tyson, come on up," she called, her voice steady despite the emotions swirling inside her. Myia took a deep breath and shared a glance with Tyson, who nodded. They walked to the front, the weight of their grief palpable but overshadowed by the love they had for their mother.

Once at the front, she placed a comforting hand on Myia's shoulder and then on Tyson's. "Thank you all for being here today to celebrate my sister's life," she began, her voice wavering slightly. "She was a remarkable woman, strong, loving, and fiercely protective of her family. We have lost so much, but today, we honor her memory."

Myia stepped forward, her voice trembling but resolute. "Mom taught us to always cherish our family and friends, to stand by one another no matter what. She was our rock, and I will always remember her laughter, her kindness, and how much she believed in us."

Tears filled her eyes as she paused, looking at the crowd of familiar faces offering their support.

Tyson followed, his own heartache evident. "My mom was the best. She always made time for us, whether it was to help with homework or just to talk about our day. I wish she could be here to see all of you gathered in her honor. It means so much to me." His voice cracked but he pushed through. He knew that his mother wanted him to be strong.

As they spoke, Marcus and Jordan stood slightly off to the side listening intently. They were both deeply moved by the heartfelt words, and it brought a mix of pride and sorrow to their hearts. Just then, two figures approached the brothers. It was a pair of older men who were from one of the neighborhoods they searched in when Niyah first went missing. One of them kept turning around and looking over his shoulders, while the other seemed like he didn't want to be bothered. Marcus narrowed his eyes, unsure of their intentions.

"Hey, you're Marcus, right?" the first guy said, leaning in slightly. "We heard about the memorial and thought we'd come show our support." There was something about the way that he spoke that made Marcus feel uneasy. Jordan felt it too and looked at his brother waiting for a cue . "What do you want?" he asked bluntly, sensing that something wasn't quite right.

The first guy smirked, crossing his arms. "Just looking to talk. Thought it'd be cool to exchange a few words."

Marcus felt a surge of protectiveness wash over him. "This ain't the time or place. Not interested," he replied firmly, his gaze steely.

"Come on, man, we're just trying to help," the first guy insisted, though there was a hint of aggression in his tone. "This isn't just about your aunt anymore, you know. There's more at stake."

Jordan stepped in closer to his brother, his body tense. "You really think now is the time for this? We're here to remember our family, not deal with whatever shit you're trying to bring."

"Well if you don't want to hear what I know then we'll just go talk to your mom then. C'mon let's go," the second guy said as they turned to walk away. When they were a few yards away, Marcus suddenly heard one of them mutter something under his breath that caught his attention. "I'm not doing this for Malik. What he did wasn't right," the first guy said glancing back.

Marcus froze, his eyes narrowing in recognition. "Wait... Lonnie? Lonnie Jackson?" he asked, finally piecing it together. He'd seen Lonnie around a few times, but it had been years since they'd crossed paths.

Chapter 35

Lonnie stopped, sighing before turning fully to face the brothers. "Yeah, it's me. I'm not here to stir up trouble," he said more seriously, his tone shifting. "I knew your aunt, and I don't like what Malik did. I've got my own reasons for wanting this handled the right way."

Jordan's eyes flashed with skepticism, but Marcus could see something genuine in Lonnie's expression, something that wasn't there with the other guy. "Then why show up like this?" He asked, the suspicion still lingering in his voice.

Lonnie shrugged. "Look, I came to the memorial because I needed to pay my respects, but when I saw you, I thought I could help. Your aunt used to hang with my younger when they were young. She always looked out for her even when I was locked up. I can't repay her for what she's done but I can try to make things right. I know why y'all nor the police can find Malik." His voice was low, almost conspiratorial, like he didn't want anyone else to overhear.

The brothers exchanged glances. This was unexpected, and Marcus could feel his heart racing, torn between distrust and a strange sense of relief that they were getting closer to some answers. "Why tell us now?" Jordan asked, his voice guarded.

"Because Malik deserves what's coming to him," Lonnie said bluntly, his expression hardening. "And I'm not about to let him get away with it. I'm telling you where to find him because I don't want to see someone else pay the price for what he did. You get what I'm saying?"

Marcus nodded slowly, taking in Lonnie's words. "Where is he?"

Lonnie glanced around before speaking in a hushed tone. "He's been laying low a state over. I don't know how long he'll stay put, but I can give you the location. You'll want to act fast, though. Malik's connected. And don't let it get back to me"

Jordan looked back at the gathering, concerned about their mom or anyone else overhearing this intense conversation. "Why should we trust you now?"

Lonnie shrugged again. "I may not have always made the right choices, but Malik crossed a line that no one should. I just want to see this end the right way. Take it or leave it."

Jordan, after a long pause, nodded. "Tell us."

Marcus watched as Lonnie hesitated. He was feeling torn. On one side Malik was his boy for life. They've known each other for years but on the other hand, Niyah was the only one who looked out for his sister. He could see the internal struggle on Lonnie's face, as if he was weighing the consequences of divulging Malik's whereabouts against the risks it could pose to himself.

"Look, we don't have all day," Marcus pressed, urgency creeping into his tone. "This is about our aunt. We need to know where that piece of shit is."

Jordan shifted uneasily, glancing at the crowd gathered for the memorial. "You can't keep us hanging like this. If you know something, just spill it," he added, trying to push the man to respond.

Finally, Lonnie looked back up. "Alright, but you have to understand the risks. He may not be alone and things could get messy. You want to find Malik? He's at a motel in Woodley off Highway 65—Room 204."

Marcus's heart raced at the revelation. This was it. They finally had a lead on Malik. "What's he doing there?" he asked.

"Not sure," Lonnie replied, shaking his head. "But I wouldn't take too long getting there. I just overheard he's been planning to leave again. It's only a matter of time ."

Jordan frowned, a mix of disbelief and concern crossing his face. "And what about you? What's stopping you from just running off to him?"

"I'm not like Malik," Lonnie said firmly. "I want to do the right thing. What he did to that woman was unforgivable. I won't be part of that."

"Why now? Why not tell the police?" Marcus pressed, wanting to understand Lonnie's motives better.

"Because they might just screw it up," Lonnie replied. "And I'm not about to let that happen. I'll leave it to you to decide what to do with this information. Just remember, if you go after him, be careful. Malik is unpredictable." With that, Lonnie walked to where his friend was and they disappeared into the crowd.

Marcus felt the gravity of the moment settle in. They had a lead, but with it came a rush of adrenaline and fear. "We have to go now," he said to Jordan, his mind racing. "We can't waste any time."

"Let's tell Mom and Myia we're stepping out for a bit."

As they turned back to the memorial, Marcus could still hear the soft music playing and the laughter mingling with the sobs. The day was supposed to be about celebrating life, but now it was turning into something darker, more complicated.

"We need to handle this the right way," Marcus said quietly, steeling himself for what lay ahead. "For her."

"What's the plan when we get there," Jordan asked as they made their way through the crowd. "Didn't you hear Lonnie say that Malik's unpredictable?"

"I'll let you know on the way," he said as they maneuvered between the clusters of people sharing stories and memories of Niyah. When they were near Darren, he looked up from where he was talking with a few family friends, his brow furrowing slightly at their serious expressions.

"Hey, what's going on?" Darren asked, noting the urgency in their demeanor.

"We need to run an errand," Marcus said, keeping his voice steady but low. "We'll be back soon."

Darren studied them for a moment, a skeptical look crossing his face. "An errand? Right now? You know today's not the best time for that, right?"

Jordan exchanged a glance with Marcus, trying to gauge how to explain without revealing too much. "It's important," Jordan added, trying to sound convincing. "We promise we'll come back."

Darren crossed his arms, still looking uncertain. "I don't like the sound of this, but if you're going, just be careful, okay? There's a lot going on."

Marcus nodded, appreciating the concern but feeling the clock ticking in his mind. "We will, I promise."

With that, they turned and hurried away from the crowd and headed towards the parking lot. The atmosphere was heavy with grief, but Marcus felt a pulse of adrenaline driving him forward. This was their chance to get some answers about Malik, and he couldn't afford to let it slip away.

As they reached the car, Jordan glanced back at the memorial. "Do you think we're doing the right thing?" he asked, the weight of the moment settling on his shoulders.

"We have to," Marcus replied firmly. "We owe it to Myia and Tyson. We can't just let Malik disappear. If we can find him and bring him to justice, we'll at least be doing something."

Jordan nodded, determination flickering in his eyes. They jumped into the car, and Marcus started the engine, feeling the roar of the vehicle match the urgency coursing through him. As they pulled away from Hidden Oaks, he glanced in the rear view mirror then at Jordan. "Let's go find him."

The car was filled with a tense silence as they drove away from the park, the echoes of the memorial still lingering in their minds. Jordan stared out the window. He could still see Myia's face in his mind, her pain and grief etched so deeply it felt like his own.

"This isn't just about us," Jordan finally said, breaking the silence. "This is about giving Myia, Tyson, and even Auntie, the justice they deserve. He doesn't get to walk away from this."

"I know. But we have to be smart. No reckless moves. We don't want to mess this up or get ourselves in trouble." His tone was firm, but the tension in his voice betrayed the storm brewing inside him.

"We'll find him. One way or another, we'll make sure he pays."

Marcus didn't reply, his focus locked on the road ahead. The streets stretched out before them endless and uncertain, but their destination was clear. They wouldn't stop until they uncovered Malik's hiding place.

Chapter 36

Malik stared at the screen as the purple and white balloons drifted into the sky, their ascent slow but steady. Each one seemed to carry a piece of his guilt, the weight of the choices he'd made, the life he'd taken, and the family he'd shattered. The image of her son standing so quietly struck Malik harder than anything. That boy had lost his mother, and for what? Malik couldn't even justify it to himself anymore. He wanted to shut it all out, to turn the phone off and disappear, but he couldn't shake the feeling deep inside, gnawing at him.

He tossed the phone aside as he buried his face in his hands. He had the image of the memorial etched in his mind. A wave of nausea swept over him. He had thought about running. In fact he had been planning to. He even had the money, the fake phone, and the cash car waiting outside the motel. He could slip away, fade into the background, and no one would ever find him.

But then the memory of his son flickered in his mind. If Malik ran, then he'd be leaving behind even more. Isaiah would grow up knowing that his father wasn't just gone, but that he was a coward who couldn't face what he'd done.

Malik stood up and paced the small room. His mind had him feeling like the walls were closing in on him. He felt torn in two directions. One side was the urge to escape and start over somewhere far away. The other side was the grim realization of turning himself in and hoping that he will still have a chance to have Isaiah in his life.

He paused by the window and looked out at the deserted parking lot. His mind raced calculating the possibilities. Could he really face the police? What could he even say? Would they believe him if he said it was an accident? Probably not. And he know that Camille would never let Isaiah visit him if he ended up behind bars. He knew that for a fact.

But as he stood there conflicted watching the replay of the memorial, Malik realized something else. Running would only drag this out. Guilt and fear would follow him wherever he went. There would be no escape from what he'd done. He would spend the rest of his life looking over his shoulder, haunted by the memory of Niyah and what he'd taken from her family.

He had to decide quickly. Run and lose everything or turn himself in and face the consequences. The weight of the decision crushed him, but in his gut, he knew the answer. There was no escaping the inevitable. His voice wavered as he dialed the number he never thought he would call.

Detective Samuels answered on the second ring, his voice sharp and to the point. "Samuels."

Malik's throat felt dry, but he forced himself to speak. "It's Malik Johnson. I need to talk"

There was a pause on the other end, and Malik could almost feel the tension through the phone. "Malik. Where are you?"

"It doesn't matter," Malik said quietly. "I... I've decided to turn myself in."

Samuels' voice remained calm, but there was an unmistakable edge of surprise.

"You're making the right choice, Malik. When and where?"

Malik swallowed hard. "I'll come in tomorrow morning. I'll meet you at the station at eight."

Samuels' voice was measured, but firm. "We'll be waiting. And Malik, don't even think about running again . This is your last chance."

"You have my word," Malik said, his voice barely above a whisper. "I'll be there." The call ended, and Malik let the phone drop into his lap. His hands were shaking, but there was a strange sense of relief mixed with the fear. For the first time in weeks, he felt like he could breathe again. He knew he'd have to make one more call tonight. He can't put it off. He dialed the number and let it ring. His heart hammered in his chest as the phone rang, each second feeling like an eternity.

When his mother's voice finally came through the line, it sounded soft, strained, as though she'd been waiting for this call. "Malik where are you? Are you okay?" Her voice was full of concern like she had sensed this moment was coming. He couldn't answer her just yet. He just really wanted to hear the sound of her voice. "I saw the memorial on the news earlier. That family has to be hurting a lot right now."

He hesitated for a moment, swallowing hard. "That's why I'm calling," he started, his voice unsteady. "I'm... I'm turning myself in tomorrow morning. I can't keep running from this. I just.." his words faltered as he tried to find the right way to say it. "I just can't live like this anymore."

There was a pause, and he could hear her breathing change, the tremble in her voice evident. "Tomorrow? You're really doing this?"

"I have to," Malik said emotionally. "I've made a mess of everything, and I need to face it. I can't keep running."

His mother let out a choked sob, the sound breaking his heart all over again. "What about me? What about your son?"

"Mom I have to face this. How can I look my son in the eyes if I don't face what I've done. I can't live with myself knowing that everywhere I turn, someone would be watching me or worse. I have to do this. if not for me then for him."

His mother exhaled, the pain in her breath unmistakable. "You don't have to do this alone. You could come home now. We could figure something out like get you a lawyer ..."

"Is that Malik?" Mike's deep voice cut through the line, and Malik stiffened. He hadn't expected to hear him. He must have snatched the phone from Sandra . "What's this about turning yourself in?"

Malik clenched his jaw, his heart racing. "Yeah, Mike. It's time. I can't keep running. I messed up, and I have to face it.'"

Mike replied loudly "You're damn right you messed up. Look at the mess you've made. All this running? I know damn well you were raised better than that!"

" I know I've let you down Mike and I'm going to do what's right now. I just wanted to see you both before I go in tomorrow."

"You should've never gotten yourself in this situation in the first place," Mike muttered, and Malik could hear the frustration brewing. "You made your bed, son. Now you've got to lie in it."

There was a shuffle on the line, and Malik could hear his mother's voice in the background, pleading with his father to stop. "Just let him talk, please."

"Malik," his mother's voice came back on, softer but strained. "Come home tonight. We'll figure out what to do. You don't have to do this alone."

"I can't, Mom," Malik said quietly, his throat tight with emotion. "I'm not running anymore, but I need to think tonight. I'll stop by in the morning before I go in. I promise."

"Why wait until the morning. We'll come see you tonight. Where are you?"

"I can't tell you where I am in case someone is listening. Just trust me to show up in the morning. I need tonight to myself to make sure that I am making the right choice on my own."

"Why not come tonight?" Mike asked in the background. "If you're serious about doing the right thing, come home. We'll face this together."

"I need to be alone tonight. I'll see you guys in the morning. I just wanted to say... I'm sorry. For everything."

His mother's soft sob echoed through the line, and his stepfather's heavy sigh followed. There was no more anger, just a quiet acceptance. "Okay . We will see you in the morning bright and early. Do you want me to make you some breakfast?"

"No mom," he said exasperated. "I'll eat before I get there. Remember this is not a long visit. I want to see both your and Mike faces before I turn myself in."

"Are you sure sweetie? You know we're up early anyway..." Sandra started.

"We'll be here," Mike said. "Just don't make us wait too long."

"I won't," Malik whispered. "I'll see you two in the morning." He hung up before the tears threatened to spill, knowing that this was his final night of freedom before everything changed forever.

Malik stepped outside pulling a Black & Mild from his jacket pocket. The familiar scent of the cigarillo was comforting in a way, grounding him for a moment. He leaned against the hood of his car, cupped his hand around the lighter as he sparked it, and watched the tip flare up before taking a slow drag.

The night was quiet, but Malik's mind was anything but. He let the smoke fill his lungs, holding it in before exhaling a slow cloud into the evening air. Tomorrow, he'd turn himself in. That thought gnawed at him with every puff he took. He had no idea what to expect, but one thing was clear; this was his last night of freedom.

As he took another drag, his eyes wandered around the nearly empty parking lot. That's when he noticed it, a car parked a few spaces down. He hadn't seen it before. It was a dark sedan with two guys sitting inside. They weren't moving, just sitting there. He couldn't see anything else or rather he didn't pay attention to anything else. He barely left the room the whole two weeks he was there, only walking next door late at night to get food and drinks.

Malik's pulse quickened. He stared at the car, his thoughts spiraling. Who were they? Were they watching him? His heart raced as his mind went into overdrive. Were they working with the police? Are they here to take him in before he could even get to the station tomorrow. He flicked the Black & Mild nervously, the ash falling onto the pavement.

But then he shook his head. "Nah, man. You're trippin'," he muttered to himself. After all, it was a cheap motel. People came and went all the time. Sketchy cars and strange people were all part of the scenery. For all he knew they could be meeting up or doing what he's doing, lighting up. He took another long puff, feeling the smoke fill his chest, trying to calm his nerves.

He glanced back at the car one last time. The two men still hadn't moved. But this was a motel and nothing about this place was ever straight. He flicked the cigar to the ground crushing it under his foot before turning to head back inside. Yeah, he thought, he just wasn't going to get any sleep tonight. Might as well walk to Crossroads Cafe to get a meal. He put on his hoodie and stepped back out, the cool air hitting his face as he walked across the cracked asphalt of the parking lot. The street was quiet at this hour except for a few cars speeding by. Their headlights flickered as they cut through the fading light. He kept his head down and his hands stuffed in his hoodie pockets as he made his way toward the familiar diner.

Chapter 37

A few truckers sat at the counter, sipping coffee and talking in low voices. Malik slid into a booth by the window, his back to the street, and picked up the sticky menu. He wasn't really hungry but he needed to take his mind off of tomorrow. Looking at the options, he was trying to decide which special would help settle the nerves. As he sat there waiting for the waitress, Malik's eyes wandered to the window. His eyes scanned the motel lot across the street and he noticed that the dark sedan from earlier was gone.

Malik blinked, leaning forward slightly as if to make sure he wasn't imagining things. He didn't know how to feel about that. It was a cheap motel and the two men never got out the car. He felt uneasy about that. He tried to shake the suspicion. "It's just a coincidence," he muttered under his breath, but the nagging thought wouldn't leave him alone. "I just need to get through tonight," he whispered to himself, pulling the hood tighter over his head.

The waitress arrived, her shoes clicking against the worn linoleum as she set a cup of coffee down in front of Malik. Her smile was tight, almost like she'd seen too many weary faces pass through this diner. Her eyes lingered on him for a second too long, and he felt a prickle of discomfort. He tried to ignore it, offering a half-smile as he ordered his food, keeping his voice low. The last thing he needed was to draw attention. He glanced at the door, then back to the counter, where the truckers were still talking in low murmurs. The conversation was a blur of words about delivery routes and weather forecasts, nothing that concerned him. But their presence made him feel more isolated, like he was on the edge of something he couldn't quite see.

As he waited, his mind kept drifting back to that sedan. It had been parked outside the motel for hours, the two men sitting inside without a single glance toward the outside world. Maybe it was nothing. Maybe they were just waiting on someone. Maybe it was something else altogether. His fingers drummed against the edge of the table, a nervous habit he hadn't been able to shake since the incident. The thought of being recognized, of someone connecting him to the news coverage of Niyah's memorial, sent a cold wave of fear through him. He shoved the thought away and focused on the window again, scanning the parking lot, trying to spot anything out of the ordinary. But the sedan was gone, and the lot was empty. Still, it felt like something was lingering, like the weight of the world was pressing down on him.

The food arrived in a brown paper bag, and Malik barely looked at it as the waitress slid it across the table. He nodded quickly, handing her cash, the tip almost more generous than he meant it to be, but he didn't want to draw attention. He grabbed the bag, stood up quickly, and slipped out the door. The cool night air hit him immediately, sharp and bracing.

The walk back to the motel was just as long and tense as before, and the unease was growing, gnawing at the edges of his mind. His fingers clenched tightly around the paper bag as he crossed the street, his gaze darting down every alleyway and up to the darkened windows of the shops lining the street. His breath came out in shallow puffs, the only sound cutting through the stillness around him. Each step he took felt weighted, as though the ground itself was slowing him down, making him feel trapped. The faint rustle of trash being blown in the distance made him jump. His heart raced as he glanced around, but nothing was there. However he couldn't shake the feeling that he was being watched.

When he finally reached the motel, Malik felt a small wave of relief wash over him, though it did little to soothe his nerves. He glanced around once more, satisfied that it was still empty. He fumbled for his key, unlocked the door quickly and stepped inside. He locked, checked, and doubled checked the locks on the door. Dropping the bag of food on the table, he let out a long breath. He couldn't even enjoy the food due to the feeling that something still wasn't right. He eventually assured himself that he'd be turning himself in soon. He just needed to make it through the night.

Malik sat at the table, staring at the bag of food as if it might hold some kind of answer, some reassurance that he was making the right decision. The hum of the fluorescent light above buzzed louder in the silence, a constant reminder of how alone he felt. He hadn't even touched the food yet, his appetite long gone. Instead, his mind kept circling back to that dark sedan, its two occupants, the way they never moved nor got out. It wasn't just paranoia anymore, something was off. He could feel it, like a weight pressing down on his chest.

He stood up abruptly, pacing the small cramped room. His paranoia, or guilty conscience, was getting worse and every creak from the old motel felt like a footstep just outside the door. He went to the window, pulling back the flimsy curtain just enough to peer out into the parking lot. The sedan was gone, but that didn't make him feel any safer. What had those men been waiting for? And why had they been watching him so intently? He had no answers, only questions that dug into him deeper with every passing second.

Malik forced himself to sit back down, breathing slowly to calm his nerves. He needed to stay focused, to keep his head on straight. Tomorrow was coming whether he was ready or not. He had a plan, sort of. There was no going back, no undoing the mess he had made. But the uncertainty of it all, the nagging sense that something else was happening just beyond his reach, kept him on edge. He turned his attention to the food again, but all he could taste was the bitter tang of fear in the back of his throat. He reached for the plastic fork, but it felt like an effort just to make the motion, like even the simplest tasks required more energy than he had left to give.

His mind replayed the encounter over and over, each time it seemed more unsettling than the last. The men had been too calm, too calculated in their movements. They hadn't been searching for something. No, it had been more like they were waiting for someone, for him. The realization gnawed at him clawing its way under his skin. He knew he couldn't keep running, but the thought of staying put felt just as dangerous. Whatever this was, whatever he had stumbled into, it was far bigger than him now.

He tried to steady his breathing, forcing himself to focus. "Only one person knew where I was going", he reminded himself. "Lonnie." He trusted him with his life. Hadn't he helped him slip away when everything else was falling apart? He was the only one who knew the plan, and if anyone could be trusted in this mess, it was him. He wiped his palms on his jeans, trying to quiet the rising panic. "*They're not looking for you,*" he told himself. "*It's just a coincidence.*" But even as the words formed in his mind, a shadow of doubt lingered. What if that one thread of trust had been broken? What if he'd been wrong about everything? He glanced at the car again. The figures still hadn't moved.

The thought hit him like a jolt of ice water. What if Lonnie had put a tracker on the car? It seemed impossible, but the more he thought about it, the more it made sense. He'd always trusted him, but in this game, trust could be a dangerous thing. Maybe this so-called ally wasn't as loyal as he'd thought. Maybe the guy had figured out a way to track him, to keep tabs on his every move. But the gnawing feeling wouldn't let go. If there was a tracker on the car, it wouldn't matter how far he ran. Someone would always be a step behind. His mind was made up. He had to get out of here, and fast.

Malik's hand trembled as he reached for the small lamp on the nightstand. He had to think, had to plan; there had to be a way out of this. His mind, however, felt like it was spinning in circles, unable to grasp onto anything concrete. The world outside the motel felt distant, like it was happening in some other place, some other time. Here, in this tiny, suffocating room, he was alone with his thoughts and his fears. Every moment stretched on endlessly, each breath coming slower, more labored. He forced himself to look at the window again, but the empty parking lot offered no comfort. It only reminded him that what had happened tonight wasn't an accident. Someone was watching. Someone always would be.

Chapter 38

"Are you sure this is the place?" Marcus asked as he pulled into the motel parking lot. Jordan read the text from Lonnie "Yeah this is it. Now all we need to do is look for a beige Toyota Camry." He pulled into a close spot and they started to scan the cars in the lot.

"How do you think he knew where Malik was? Do you trust him?"

"It's too late to think about it now. Seems like he's telling the truth so far. Look over there."

Jordan leaned forward. "There it is," he said pointing to it a few spaces down. "That's definitely Malik's ride."

"Alright, now we just need to figure out which room he's in."

"How do we know it's not a setup for us? After all, we both know Lonnie can't be trusted."

"Look if you don't want to do this, then just stay your ass in the car."

"It ain't that. Why don't we just call the police and let them know where he is?"

"And what do you think will happen? They will pick him up and he will get off with a lawyer since his face is all over the news anyway. And that means no justice for us. How do you think Mom will feel about that? Or even Myia or Tyson?"

"Okay okay okay. You made your point. Are we going to just knock on each door by the car? I just know we ain't gonna check in this place." Jordan said looking at the entrance. "I wouldn't be caught dead here."

"No. We'll sit here and watch the doors. Eventually he will come out for something." Marcus answered. "He could come out at any moment."

They sat in silence for an hour. All that could be heard was the sound of traffic on the highway. Jordan broke the silence. "What if he doesn't come out soon? I'm getting hungry and I gotta take a piss. " The words hung in the air for a moment, cutting through the tension.

"That's all you think about isn't it. There's a Crossroads Cafe across the street. We can stop there or we can stop somewhere else on the way back." Jordan shrugged, glancing over at his brother with a mix of frustration and resignation. "I'm just saying, we've been sitting here forever, and I'm not gonna starve for some guy who we can't guarantee that he'll leave his room."

They were there for another two hours before Marcus suggested, "If he doesn't leave his room in the next thirty minutes, then we'll head back." Jordan let out a sharp sigh, rubbing his eyes in exhaustion. "Fine," he muttered, "but if we don't leave soon, I'm just gonna eat over there and pretend this whole thing never happened." No sooner than he could get the words our of his mouth, he exclaimed "Wait! Look over there at 204. Isn't that him?"

Marcus turned sharply and there was Malik, stepping out of the room wearing a black hoodie. He seemed tense looking around nervously, his eyes darting as if he was expecting something. "Yep that's that piece of shit. Let's see what he's doing. Be still and don't bring any attention our way."

Jordan's grip tightened on the door handle. "What do we do now?"

"We wait. Let's see where he's headed. He doesn't know we're here."

The brothers watched as Malik walked to his car, leaned against the hood and lit a cigar. He took a slow drag and surveyed the parking lot as if he were enjoying the night. Marcus's phone buzzed in his lap. He glanced down half expecting it to be something routine, but when he opened the message, his heart skipped a beat.

It was from Lonnie.

"He's turning himself in tomorrow morning. That's the word on the street."

Marcus stared at the screen for a moment, the news sinking in. He wasn't sure whether to feel relieved or more frustrated. After all this time, after everything Malik had put them through, now he was just going to turn himself in like it was nothing? It didn't feel like enough. It didn't feel like justice.

"What is it?" Jordan asked, noticing the shift in Marcus's expression. He handed him the phone without saying a word. His brother read the message, his face hardening. "So, that's it? He's just gonna turn himself in, and we're supposed to sit here and let that happen?"

"Nah. I'm not about to let him walk into that station like everything's good. He doesn't deserve that. He took my aunt away from us."

"Why is he just hanging out there?" Jordan wondered, frowning. "He doesn't seem in any rush."

"Looks like he's waiting for someone," Marcus suggested, glancing at that direction. "Or he's just trying to keep a low profile. Either way, we can't let him see us." Malik casually scanned the area again, and for a moment, it seemed like his gaze lingered in their direction. Marcus held his breath, heart racing, but Malik turned back to the cigar, seemingly oblivious.

"Do you think he saw us?" Jordan asked.

"I can't tell. Let's see if he goes back inside or if someone else shows up."

As they waited, Malik took his time, enjoying the smoke and the cool night air. Every second felt like an eternity, but they remained focused, determined to figure out what he was up to. Finally, Malik flicked the cigar butt onto the pavement, crushing it underfoot. He straightened up, glancing around once more before heading back toward the room.

"Okay, he didn't recognize us," Jordan said, letting out a relieved breath. "But we still can't just sit here forever."

"Agreed," Marcus said, keeping his gaze fixed on Malik. "Let's go eat and check in with the others."

"What about him?"

"If he's turning himself in tomorrow morning. That gives us tonight. We can stop him before he gets there."

"You sure about that?"

"Yeah. We can't just sit here and let him control how this ends."

The brothers sat in the car for a long moment, exchanging a few quiet words. They had been watching him closely, noting every nervous glance, every small twitch of his body. Something about him seemed off, too cautious, too aware. Marcus made a quick call, then glanced over. "Let's check in at the motel down the road," he said, his voice low. "We'll keep an eye on him tonight, then follow him in the morning."

They turned into a small weathered motel with a flickering neon sign that buzzed intermittently. It wasn't much just a low building with peeling paint and a few tired cars parked outside, but it would do. They parked in the back away from the main entrance, and slipped inside to check in under fake names. They took a room on the second floor, their view of the street offering a perfect vantage point. They sat in silence for a while, the hum of the air conditioning filling the space between them. Jordan finally asked, "What's the plan?"

"Let's wait until morning," Marcus said. "Then we'll follow him. See where he goes next."

They had one shot at this. One chance to stop Malik before he made his move. The weight of the decision pressed down on him, but he wasn't about to second guess it now. He couldn't afford to. Malik was a liability, and if they didn't act fast, everything they had worked for could unravel before their eyes. Jordan had his doubts, but he wasn't about to voice them. Marcus had made his choice and Jordan was with him, at least for now. There was no going back after this, no undoing what they were about to do. He glanced at his older brother, catching a glimpse of the grim determination in his eyes. It was a look he knew all too well. They had both crossed lines before, but this... this felt different. As the night progressed, he couldn't shake the feeling that they were heading into something far worse than they had anticipated.

Chapter 39

Inside his motel room, Malik moved quickly, his movements sharp and deliberate. He checked the small clock on the nightstand. It was just before dawn. Today was the day he would face the music. After everything, he couldn't run anymore. He had to face the consequences of his actions, even if it meant he would lose his freedom. It was time to go. He had to keep moving

After a quick shower he dressed in a simple t-shirt and jeans, the familiar fabric offering some comfort. He grabbed his duffel bag, stuffing it with the few essentials he'd brought, his eyes flicking to the door every few seconds as though expecting someone to burst in. He'd stayed in that room long enough. Too long, maybe. He didn't trust it, didn't trust the sense that something was off. The figures in the car the previous night were still on his mind, their faces hidden, but their presence too deliberate to ignore. He gave a quick glance around the room, the place that was his own little personal prison the last couple of weeks.

Malik took a deep breath as he stepped outside to his car. He tried to calm the anxiety that was building up inside. He shoved the bag into the backseat of his car, making sure everything was locked tight. No room for mistakes. As he headed to checkout, he glanced over his shoulder, eyes narrowing in the dim light. The place felt quiet, eerily quiet. He didn't know why, but he had the distinct feeling he was being watched. With one last glance back at the motel, he pulled out onto the road and headed toward his parents' house.

Unseen by him, the two brothers in the motel down the street were already awake, watching from their room, their eyes trained on Malik moving between the cars. They could see his every move, the way he was checking his surroundings. They were waiting.

"He's leaving," Jordan whispered, his voice steady.

Malik nodded, leaning forward. "Stay close. Let's see which way he is headed."

They both knew the game was changing now. The morning was just starting, but the chase was already on.

Malik turned on the radio but he couldn't get into the music. He tried an audio book and a podcast. They didn't work either so he continued driving in silence. He tried to concentrate but his thoughts and actions kept replaying in his mind. *"This is going to be a long drive"*, he thought. There weren't that many cars on the road that morning. He had to think of something that would calm his mind. Then he remembered the game that he and Isaiah would play on road trips. One of them would count the number of 18 wheelers and the other one would count the cars with out of state plates. His heart twisted at the memory.

How long had it been since he'd seen him? Since he'd last held him in his arms, played with him?

Isaiah deserved more than the life he was living, more than the weight of his father's choices. And yet, the ache in his chest wouldn't go away. He'd failed his son in ways that couldn't be undone, and now he was about to give himself up, knowing he could never make it right. Malik knew that this would be his last road trip for awhile, if ever.

He saw the sign that said Crest Ridge 80 miles and was now second guessing the decision to turn himself in. He could always get off on the next exit and drive the other way. Suddenly, a jarring thud interrupted his thoughts. The car lurched, and he heard the unmistakable sound of a tire losing air. Malik cursed under his breath as the wheel wobbled. He quickly pulled over to the side of the road, the tire completely flat. He looked around, trying to get his bearings, before letting out a frustrated sigh.

Malik cursed under his breath as the car jerked, and the wheel wobbled. He quickly pulled over to the side of the road to see what was the issue. Stepping out, he assessed the damage. The passenger rear tire was completely flat, a nasty gash visible on the side. He could have sworn that he didn't run over anything and when he checked the car earlier all of the tires looked good for travel. Besides he didn't go anywhere the whole time he was at the motel. "Just what I needed," he said walking to the trunk. "This is going to be a long day."

With a sigh, he opened the trunk and pulled out the spare and the tools he needed. He wasn't in the mood for this and the thought of having to change a flat in this moment felt like just another cruel twist of fate. His hands were shaky as he jacked up the car and pulled the wheel off. He was concentrating on changing the spare that he didn't notice the sedan pulling in behind him.

Malik continued changing the tire. Before he could put the lug nuts on, he heard the sound of two doors open and close. Footsteps crunched against the gravel, slow but deliberate and it sent a chill up his spine. "Hey man, you need any help?" the stranger asked.

"I'm straight," Malik said without looking up. "I'm almost done. Thanks for stopping." The man didn't move. He just stood there. Malik continued, "I'm going to finish changing the tire and then I'll be on my way. Again thanks for offering to help." He heard another set of footsteps approached and stopped at the trunk. By the time he glanced up it was too late. The sharp crack of metal against skull echoed in the morning air, and Malik's vision exploded in red hot pain. He barely had time to react before he felt the metal again. He saw the world getting dark.

The tire iron hit him a third time knocking his back to the ground with a heavy thud. His hands instinctively reached up to his head, but his vision was already spinning. The pain was too much for him to focus. He collapsed, dazed, his body slumping to the side as blood began to trickle from the wound on his forehead.

Malik rolled onto his stomach and tried to push himself up, but he wasn't fast enough. Another blow landed, this time on his leg. Pain radiated through him forcing a choked cry through his lips. The blows just continued to come each one harder than the previous one.

"Get up!" the attacker said menacingly.

"Who are you?" Malik winced. He looked up and was staring at the two men as they stood over him. Their faces were unreadable. Neither of them said a word.

Both men were wearing dark clothes, ski masks, and black gloves. The one with the tire iron had a muscular build while the other one was slim. He tried to think of if he met them before but nothing came to mind. Then he saw the car behind them. He had seen the car before but he couldn't remember if it was in passing, or if it was due to his paranoia.

Then he remembered he saw the car last night at the motel. So he wasn't paranoid then. They were looking for him. Now he just need to figure out fast who sent them. No one knew where he went. So how did they find out the exact motel he was staying in? He couldn't think about that now. He had to get away from here and see his mom before turning himself in. forced himself to steady his breathing, eyeing the man with the tire iron as he took a small step back. "Look, I don't know who you are or what you want. If this is about money..." His words fell short as the other stranger raised a gloved finger to his lips, signaling for silence. Malik swallowed hard, the taste of fear settling in his throat. He knew then that this wasn't about money, nor was it random. These men had a purpose, one that he was just beginning to comprehend, and it was too late to escape it.

The attacker started to laugh, a cruel laughter that echoed. "Someone who wants you to get what you deserve," he said, raising the tire iron again. Malik's heart raced as he processed the words. "What does that even mean?" he shouted.

"It means your past is catching up with you," the man sneered stepping closer, the tire iron glinting ominously in the sunlight. "Time to pay the price."

With that he swung a final blow, the sickening sound of impact echoing in the morning air as Malik crumpled to the ground, motionless. The stranger stood over him for a moment, chest heaving with the remnants of his effort, but his face remained cold and unaffected. He took off his mask and wiped the sweat off his forehead. He crouched beside Malik's body, his eyes scanning the lifeless form for a moment longer. His breathing was steady and controlled, despite the surge of adrenaline rushing through his veins. He'd done this before. It wasn't the first time, and it wouldn't be the last. His gaze flicked up briefly toward his accomplice, who stood a short distance away, eyes darting nervously as he kept watch for any signs of trouble.

"This is for Niyah," he whispered under his breath, his voice flat and cold as he gazed down at Malik's lifeless body, the blood already soaking into the pavement. There was no remorse in his words, only a grim sense of finality. His partner standing a few feet away, barely acknowledged the whisper. "Let's see how long before they find your body," he said in an almost clinical tone. It wasn't a warning. It was just the way things were. He motioned for his partner to join him, and without a word the two of them began walking toward the car.

Once inside they sat in silence, the hum of the engine the only sound as they glanced back one last time. The look at Malik was brief, like a flicker of recognition, but there was no satisfaction, no relief. It was just another step in the cold chain of events. The lookout put the car in gear, and with a sharp twist of the wheel, they drove off, the sunrise swallowing them up as the road stretched out ahead. Behind them, the body of Malik lay forgotten by the world.

Chapter 40

Sandra's hand trembled as she clutched the phone, her stomach in knots. A week had passed since she last heard from him, when he said he'd come by in the morning to turn himself in. He never showed up. She had left countless messages, each one more desperate than the last, but her phone remained silent. And now, she had no choice but to do the thing she'd been dreading. She had to report her son missing.

Her breath caught in her throat as she dialed the number, the weight of the decision pressing down on her chest. The phone rang several times before a voice on the other end picked up.

"Crest Ridge Police Department, how can I help you?"

Sandra swallowed hard, her voice barely above a whisper. "I'd like to report my son missing. His name is Malik Johnson." There was a pause on the other end of the line, then the officer's tone shifted. "Ma'am, please hold for a moment."

She heard the line click as she was placed on hold. Her heart raced. Why did he need to transfer her? What was happening? A few moments later, another voice came through the line, one she didn't recognize but could tell was different. "Mrs. Johnson? This is Detective Samuels."

Sandra's stomach churned as the weight of the detective's name settled over her. *Detective Samuels.* She had heard that name before, in gossip conversations, on the news, and in whispers between her friends. He was the one leading the investigation into Niyah's death, the case that had never quite let go of her son, Malik. It felt like a cruel twist of fate that now, in this moment, she was the one being called, or rather, dragged back into that nightmare she thought she could escape. Her throat tightened, and for a moment she struggled to find her voice.

"Detective?" Sandra's voice cracked. "I'm calling because I haven't heard from Malik. He promised he'd come home, but it's been a week and I haven't heard from him. I'm scared. I think something's happened to him."

There was a long silence on the other end of the line. When Detective Samuels finally spoke, his voice was slow and careful.

"Mrs. Johnson... I'm sorry, but I need to tell you something difficult. Malik's body was found yesterday."

The world around Sandra went numb, the words echoing in her mind, but nothing seemed to sink in. *Malik's body. Malik was dead.* The weight of the finality hit her like a punch to the gut, and she sank back in her chair, struggling to breathe. Tears welled up in her eyes as she let out a sob, her mind reeling. Malik had been on the run, lost, but now... he was gone. She could hardly breathe, the weight of it crashing down on her

Samuels continued gently. "We're still piecing everything together, but I wanted to make sure you knew before it was on the news." She dropped the phone, sinking to her knees, her sobs filling the quiet house.

Sandra sat frozen, numb to the world around her. She felt as if her whole body had been submerged in ice, her fingers tingling as the shock set in. It couldn't be real. Not Malik. Her baby boy, who had once held her hand as they walked to the corner store, begging for candy with that wide, innocent smile. She could still remember the way his little fingers wrapped around hers, his laughter filling the air. Now, he was gone.

She didn't know how long she sat there, staring blankly ahead, until she felt a hand on her shoulder. It was her husband Mike. She didn't hear him come in the room. He heard her scream when he came home and rushed to her side. Mike knelt beside her, a look of sorrow on his face, as if he could feel the weight of her pain. He pulled Sandra into a gentle embrace, whispering, "I'm so sorry, honey. I'm so, so sorry."

Sandra sank into her husband's arms, her body trembling as the floodgates opened. The sobs came in ragged bursts, deep, raw cries that she hadn't let herself make until now. For a moment, she couldn't breathe, couldn't think beyond the suffocating pain in her chest. Malik was gone. Her son, her baby, was dead. The world felt like it was crumbling around her, each piece of it falling away as she struggled to hold on to something, anything, that could make sense of this. But nothing made sense. Not the phone call. Not the detective's words. Not the way everything she had ever known seemed to be unraveling before her eyes.

Mike held her tighter, his face buried in her hair, his own quiet sobs mixing with hers. She could feel his tears soaking into her skin and it brought her a strange comfort, as though their shared grief could make the unbearable a little more bearable. But even as he comforted her a knot twisted in her gut, a question that she had been too afraid to ask. *What had Malik gotten mixed up in?* She could sense Mike's unease, the way he was holding her so tightly, like he was trying to keep them both from falling apart completely. He had always been the protector, the one who made everything feel safe. But now, there was nothing safe. Not anymore.

The news broke the next morning. Myia was at the kitchen table when her phone lit up with a news alert. She was shocked when she read the headline:

"**Body of Malik Johnson, Suspect in Niyah Thompson Case, Found by State Trooper.**"

Her breath caught in her throat as she clicked on the link. The article described how a state trooper came across an abandoned car on the highway. When he pulled over to run the registration, that was when he found the body. It wasn't clear where Malik had been hiding, but the report said that the body looked to be dead for a couple of days.

She quickly sent a message to Marcus. *"Did you see the news? They found Malik's body"*

A minute later, her phone buzzed with his reply. *"Yeah. Been knew. Lmk if you need anything."*

Myia sat back on the couch, the phone still clutched in her hand as she stared at the screen. Her eyes scanned the message again, as if searching for some hidden meaning in the cold, distant words. *"Been knew."* What did that even mean? She'd seen his indifference before, the way he shut down when things got too close to the truth, but this felt different. It was like he was saying he already knew the worst, like Malik's death was just another piece in a story he had already read and closed the book on. Myia's mind raced as she tried to piece it together. He knew something about Malik that could change everything.

Her breath hitched as a thought took hold of her. *What if her favorite cousin was involved?* The idea made her stomach churn, but she couldn't shake it. He had always been there for her making them have an unbreakable bond. But how much did she really know her cousin? Is he really capable of doing something like that and when would he have the time? Her heart hammered in her chest, the feeling of betrayal creeping in, but she tried to push it aside. It wasn't like him to get tangled up in something like this... was it?

She quickly typed a reply, her fingers trembling slightly as she tried to make sense of her thoughts.

"*What do you mean? What do you know?*"

But even as she hit send she felt a shift in the air, as if her question was already too late. As if the truth she was about to uncover could never be something she could unhear, unsee, or forget. Myia's message delivered, the screen stayed dark for a beat too long. Her pulse quickened, anticipation tangling with dread. Then, the three dots appeared, flickering as he typed.

Finally, his reply came in:

"*Some things are better left alone, Myia.*"

Her breath caught, an ache spreading through her chest as his words settled in. She wanted to believe there was another explanation, one that didn't point to Marcus. But his silence and those words hung heavy, closing around her like a whisper she couldn't escape.

www.ingramcontent.com/pod-product-compliance
Lightning Source LLC
Chambersburg PA
CBHW071558110726
47908CB00007B/2153